The
Escape

BOOKS BY GENE EDWARDS

IN A CLASS BY ITSELF
The Divine Romance

INTRODUCTION TO THE DEEPER CHRISTIAN LIFE
Living by the Highest Life
The Secret to the Christian Life
The Inward Journey

BOOKS ON INNER HEALING
A Tale of Three Kings
The Prisoner in the Third Cell
Letters to a Devastated Christian
Climb the Highest Mountain
Exquisite Agony
(formerly titled Crucified by Christians)
Dear Lillian

RADICAL BOOKS FOR RADICAL CHRISTIANS
Overlooked Christianity
Rethinking Elders
Revolution: The Story of the Early Church
How to Meet in Homes
Beyond Radical

THE FIRST-CENTURY DIARIES
The Silas Diary
The Titus Diary
The Timothy Diary
The Priscilla Diary
The Gaius Diary

THE CHRONICLES OF HEAVEN
The Beginning
The Escape
The Birth
The Triumph
The Return

THE CHRONICLES OF
HEAVEN

Gene Edwards

SeedSowers Publishing
Jacksonville, Florida

Library of Congress Cataloging-in-Publication Data

Edwards, Gene
    The Escape : The Chronicles of Heaven / Gene Edwards
        p.   cm.
    ISBN 0-940232-99-5
    1. Jesus Christ - Nativity - Fiction. 2. Bible. N.T. History of
Biblical events - Fiction. I. Title.

SeedSowers Publishing
P.O. Box 3317
Jacksonville, FL 32206
800-228-2665
www.seedsowers.com

PROLOGUE

Abram!

It was the voice of God calling through the portal of heaven to a man being served his noon meal by a servant.

"The man doesn't hear the voice of God," observed an astonished Gabriel.

"He hears," replied the Lord. "He has been asking to hear my voice for years now."

The servant handed his master another serving of pork. The man, more pensive than a few minutes before, refused.

Obviously distracted by his own thoughts, the man began to pick disinterestedly at his food.

"He is struggling within himself, is he not?" inquired Michael.

Once more the Lord called out to the Semite.

Abram!

PART

I

CHAPTER
One

Abram raised a bit of pork, considered it, and dropped it back on his plate.

"Look at yourself," he murmured aloud. "An entire mountain covered with your cattle. And they are but one day's slaughter. My livestock reaches beyond the sight of the eye. Sheep, pigs, goats, and cattle without number. All Ur depends on my herds. Gold, silver, more than three hundred servants. I am one of the richest men in Chaldea. Still—"

"My lord."

The voice was that of one of his most trusted servants. Abram took a deep breath and sighed heavily.

"You have the final accounting?"

"Yes, lord. Yesterday we slaughtered some five thousand sheep, two thousand pigs, and eleven thousand cows. All will be ready for market by tomorrow. The mountains are exceptionally cool. The curing is excellent. There will be no spoilage. Today's

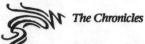

slaughter will be about the same. Shall I send a messenger into Ur to alert the merchants?"

Abram nodded.

Just then Abram bolted upright!

CHAPTER
Two

"Did someone call my name?"

Cautiously, Abram looked about in all directions, then waited. Somewhat distraught, he sat down again.

"That is the second time. The first I thought to be but the howling mountain air. But . . ."

Then, for reasons he did not understand, Abram rose to his feet and began walking toward a path that led into the upper woodlands. Once out of earshot of his servants, Abram called out softly, "Hello?"

Embarrassed, he looked around to assure himself that no one had seen him addressing the air!

Nothing. Abram continued up the path until he came to the mountain's crest. To the north and west he could see the plains of the Chaldees stretching out toward Babylon. To the south lay Ur, its ziggurat clearly visible rising from the city's center.

Staring at the ziggurat, Abram wondered aloud, "Have the gods called to me from out of the ziggurat temple?"

Abram!

Both afraid and exhilarated, Abram whirled in a complete circle, but there was no one to be found.

"Have the gods spoken to me? Will the longing finally end? Who are you?"

I am the Lord, your God . . .
Creator of heaven and earth.
Go with your father as he departs Ur.
When you have obeyed my voice,
then shall I speak to you again.

Abram waited. "Is that all?" he asked nervously.

"Is that all?" he queried again, this time with less agitation but more anxiety.

"Who are you?" he called to the winds.

The voice came again, quieter than before.

I am the Lord your God.

The Chaldean was about to call out again, but was brought short.

"Abram!"

Abram whirled around again, only to discover the voice belonged to one of his servants.

"My lord. Your father has come up from Ur. He desires to know your answer. Will you go with him as he leaves Ur and travels westward?"

"Prepare food for my father. And tell him that I have just now come to my decision."

CHAPTER
Three

Not many days thence, Abram departed Chaldea with his father, traveling as far as Haran, where Abram's father died.

After some time, Abram moved on westward toward the Great Sea, coming to a land called Canaan. In these days Lot, a nephew of Abram who lived in Sodom, was kidnapped. That event led to a battle between Abram and the kidnappers. This battle, in turn, caused the Lord to call for the gathering together of the entire population of the heavens.

CHAPTER
Four

Rarely did the entire heavenly host come together as one, and all such gatherings were memorable, loved by both God and angels. When the host of the heavenly beings was finally gathered, the Lord rose from the throne. The angelic host responded by forming a vast semicircle around the throne, while seraphim hovered above.

"I have not sensed such excitement since the day our Lord created Red Earth," whispered one of the angels, Adorae by name.

"Nor I," came the tart reply of Rathel, an angel so fierce that his disposition had birthed a proverb: "Rathel would draw his sword on Azell."

At that moment, the Lord turned toward the recording angel and pointed to the Book of Records. The most venerable of the angels raised his golden pen. With that, the Lord spoke.

As surely as I,
the Lord God,
began my Purpose with unfallen Adam,

> *today I begin again*
> *with a Gentile named Abram.*
> *This day I will make a vow to Abram,*
> *establishing a covenant with him . . .*
> *a covenant that shall be . . .*

The Lord paused.

Adorae raised one hand high above his head, ready to greet the next words of his Lord with a powerful burst of praise. True to his reputation, Rathel reached for his sword.

> *This* covenant shall be . . .
> *eternal!*

Recorder's pen faltered.

CHAPTER
Five

A covenant with man? Capricious, undependable, fallen man! thought Recorder.

"An *eternal* covenant?" came a throaty whisper from Adorae. "That presses my spirit to believe!" he declared.

"What news!" agreed Rathel, slapping his scabbard. "Back to dealing with earth and man."

"But an *eternal* covenant?" repeated a barely convinced Adorae.

"My covenant shall be established upon an *everlasting* life."

There are only two everlasting lives. As long as angels live, so will this covenant live, thought Rathel, even as a tumultuous crescendo of angelic praises broke forth, none more exuberant than Adorae's.

"Does this make angels responsible for the keeping of the covenant with man? We angels do have enemies . . . and *equals!*" mused Recorder softly.

The answer to the angels' wonderings came sure and clear. And astounding.

"The covenant will be forever. Its fulfillment rests on me alone. *I* am the keeper of the covenant."

Once more the angels rejoined in acclamations, with the usually serious Rathel leading the crescendo.

"Now hear me, my companions. A battle has taken place upon the bright blue ball that has great import. This battle began among the city kings near the Salt Sea. Abram was drawn into this conflict when his kinsman Lot was captured. With this rescue also came the liberation of *the city of Salem.*

> *Come, sons of the light,*
> *gather at the Door.*
> *There behold the conclusion*
> *of this matter*
> *and the **beginning***
> *of the **everlasting** covenant.*

CHAPTER
Six

"Thank you for helping us, Abram, and for recovering our goods. Now keep all the spoil."

The king of Sodom spoke for all the city kings Abram had assisted.

"Had it not been for your god, we all would have perished."

Abram flashed anger, responding with words white hot.

> *You confessed with your mouth*
> *that the Lord alone*
> *is the Most High God.*
> *Yet your heart allows not*
> *that you believe your words.*
> *You worship gods*
> *that are no gods.*
> *Shall I take your spoils,*
> *then hear you say,*
> *"I made Abram rich"?*
> *Shall you take glory*
> *from the God of heaven and earth?*

Be gone!
And your spoils with you!

A bemused Recorder, noting this event, could not help but include these words. "We have not often heard such defense of our Lord coming from the mouth of a fallen man."

The next entry Recorder placed into the Book of Records came from the Lord. They were words that struck terror in the spirits of the heavenly host.

"It is the hour in which I must visit the fallen planet and meet with Abram, face to face."

"That cannot be," choked Rathel. "No mortal can see the face of God and live."

"At least not since the fall," agreed a stunned Adorae.

"This day Abram has declared me to a heathen world, and he has worshiped me. Today the priesthood that is established in heaven I shall establish on earth! *The* priesthood. The priesthood that flows out of my own loins shall come to earth. And, one day, that priesthood shall be central at Salem . . . until the two be . . ."

The Lord's eyes flashed divine fire as he continued. "Heaven and earth shall become one in that city."

It was Adorae who led the shout of praise.

Heaven and earth
reunited
The seen and the unseen

*one
once more.
The dream of angels,
the consummation of
the will of God.*

Even as the anthem of praise rose in glory, the Lord, leaving the throne, moved forward until he stood upon the threshold of the Door. There, angels beheld something never seen before.

The Lord God, while passing through the Door, had taken the form of *man!*

*God became visible,
clothed in the vestments
of a human being.
What manner of meeting
does this foretell?*

At that moment, the Lord beckoned to Michael.

"Come with me. Bring with you two from among your charge. There must be messengers who know this man Abram well."

In the meantime, Recorder found himself writing furiously, valiantly trying to retain composure in a moment of astounding revelation.

The Lord God has taken upon himself the form of man, stepped upon the earth, wearing the vestments of a priest, and now . . . walks upon a dusty road toward

Abram. With him are three from among the heavenly host: Michael, Adorae, and Rathel.

But more!

Our Lord has carried with him, for the first time in all records, something out of the heavens and brought it to earth. Is our God about to give something of the riches of the heavenlies to a man? Is this a foregleam of future things?

And what will happen when God and fallen man meet . . . face to face?

CHAPTER
Seven

Abram was inspecting a herd of pigs to decide their value before selling them to an Amorite merchant. Out of the corner of his eye, he caught a glimpse of a strange man coming toward him from out of the distance.

"I know who he is!" cried Abram, striking into a full run even as he spoke.

"It is the Living God! I *know* it is he. This time I shall *see* him.

"I know you!" cried Abram as the space between the two of them closed. "You are not of this earth. You come from places not temporal. As is your realm, so also are you."

Abram paused, startled at the sight of the man's garment. "You are a priest?"

The One whom Abram rushed toward now rushed toward him. Abram's heart stopped, for he had not expected this . . . the Living God anxious to meet *him!* Not knowing what else to do, he dropped to his knees in a cloud of dust, covering his face with his hands.

> *I am the Priest of Peace.*
> *I am of Salem.*

With terror and joy mingling in his heart, Abram dared look up. Terror turned to astonishment. His God was spreading a cloth right in the middle of the road, and on the cloth a meal.

What does this mean? wondered a very confused cattleman. *The cloth . . . is it my shroud? What means this food?*

The old man's confusion now turned to amazement. The Lord of heaven and earth sat down and motioned for Abram to dine with him.

> *I, Melchizedek,*
> *whose order is forever,*
> *present this bread and wine to you,*
> *brought from realms*
> *of which you know nothing.*

And so it came about that for the very first time (but not the last), God and man sat down together, dined together, and fellowshiped together.

As Recorder inscribed this unique event, he could not but recall that long ago, in the garden, God and man had come together as unhindered as today. He also recalled the words spoken to Adam on that day. "Like you, this garden is two realms joined. Of the trees and herbs, partake for your bodies. Of the river and of the tree, partake for your spirits. And dwell

here with me, eternally. . . . Be careful what you eat.
And guard the garden."

This, and this
alone
shall make you full,
complete.
The Tree of Life
its fruit for you to eat.

Abram suddenly dismissed himself and scrambled off to find a certain one of his servants. When he returned, he carried with him a large cask filled with gold and precious stones, a tenth of all his wealth.

Abram laid the cask at the feet of Melchizedek, bowing his head as he did. When he raised his head again, his Lord had vanished, taking Abram's gift with him.

Despite his searchings and protestations, Abram realized instantly that his encounter with God had come to an end.

"A most momentous day!" observed a wonder-filled Michael to his companions. "God has brought spiritual blessings from heavenly places, made them visible, and gave them to mere man. On this same day man has presented a gift to his Lord, a gift now being brought to heavenly places."

"A most momentous day indeed!" enjoined Adorae and Rathel.

"But why were we asked to come to this strange meeting?" inquired Rathel.

"I do not know," replied Michael, "but we will find out soon enough."

As the Lord and his three companions passed back through the Door, he placed the cask into the hands of Michael.

Today has man
laid up in heaven
treasures,
for he has partaken
of the spiritual.
He gave of earth
a gift,
which into the Garden goes,
and in going there
changes the gift
the giver
and
the Garden.
So shall it be
until that day!

While a puzzled Michael carried earthly goods and laid them in the center of the Garden, near the Tree of Life, Abram, still standing in the middle of a dusty road, threw back his head, raised open hands to the skies, and bellowed, "I have seen him! I have met the

Lord of all. At last! On this day have I met him . . . face to face. My Lord and my God."

Having placed the gold and silver and costly stones in the Garden, Michael found himself dumbfounded at the results of this simple action. Not knowing what else to do, he rushed to tell his ancient friend, the recording angel.

"Recorder. I would not come to you in your duties except for a most remarkable occurrence. The Garden. I was just there."

Recorder did not so much as acknowledge Michael's presence, but continued on in his writing.

Michael persisted. "The Garden, Recorder, it—"

"I also noticed."

"But, Recorder. The Garden, it has changed. Only a little, but it has changed. It appears that it is becoming—"

"Yes, this too, I noticed," replied Recorder.

"These are wondrous times," breathed a still wide-eyed Michael.

"Tomorrow may be more so," responded the ever-stoic Recorder.

CHAPTER
Eight

All morning Abram had been haggling with the Amorite.

"I do not trust this man, or *any* Amorite. And he does not trust me. How will we ever reach an end to this bickering?"

The two men were locked in argument over the price of a hundred sheep, two hundred pigs, and five cows that the Amorite wished to purchase. By late afternoon they had, hopefully, come to a tenuous agreement. To settle the matter, there would also need to be the passing of a good sum of silver from the Amorite to Abram, along with a few goats. Abram, in turn, had to mollify the Amorite with several horses.

But a new problem arose. The dispute was now over *when* the horses would be delivered. The Amorite had promised the goats on the morrow, but he wanted the horses today. Abram was adamant that his livestock would not be delivered until the arrival of the silver and the goats.

The Amorite finally but contemptuously agreed, adding bitterly, "Hebrew!"

That settled, the Amorite called for all of his servants to stand by his side. Abram, in turn, called forth several of his servants. Together the two men spoke loudly to these gathered witnesses, calling out the nature of the bargain.

Then came the time to seal the covenant between the two men.

Abram brought forth a three-year-old heifer; the Amorite brought forth a three-year-old female goat and a three-year-old ram. Abram produced a turtledove; the Amorite, a pigeon. Together, the two men slaughtered the heifer, the goat, and the ram, slicing each animal down the middle into two equal pieces. Abram laid one half of the ram, the goat, and the heifer on one side of the ground, while the Amorite laid his half of the three animals on the other side. The birds, killed, remained uncut, one lying on Abram's side, the other at the feet of the Amorite.

The two men walked to the opposite ends of the narrow path that lay between the divided animals. Abram held up a torch; the Amorite lit a similar one. Torch in hand, Abram walked through the middle of the divided animals until he came to the side of the Amorite. The Amorite likewise walked from his place through the narrow path between the sundered animal parts until he stood in the place where Abram had stood a moment earlier.

"The covenant is established!" cried the Amorite. All of Abram's servants responded in agreement.

"The covenant is established!" cried Abram. All the Amorite servants voiced their agreement.

"I bear one half of the responsibilities of this covenant," declared Abram.

"And I the other half," responded the Amorite.

With that, the two men symbolically exchanged a few livestock and agreed to meet the following day to bring their transaction to completion.

That evening Abram, exhausted from the day's heat and the stress of dealing with the Amorite, went to his tent to rest. As he was about to fall asleep, he heard a voice.

I am the Almighty God.
This day I will also make a covenant.
It shall be between you and me.
This is my covenant:
I will multiply your seed
exceedingly.
You shall be the father
of a multitude of nations.
Therefore, from this day
you shall not be called Abram,
but Abraham,
the father of nations.
From out of your loins,
Abraham,
shall come nations and kings.

I give to you,
uncircumcised Gentile,
an everlasting covenant.
I am God to you
and to all of those
who come forth from your seed.
And to your seed
I give all this land.

Struggling to wrest himself from his stupor, Abraham heard himself reply, "How shall I know these things will come to pass?"

"We shall seal this covenant."

"A covenant, Lord? A covenant between you and me, establishing each of our responsibilities?"

"Yes. Get now a three-year-old heifer, a three-year-old goat, and a three-year-old ram. Likewise, a turtle dove and a young pigeon. Arrange them on the ground."

Abraham did so. Then, struggling as he might, he could not prevent himself from falling into a deep, troubled sleep.

"I can see nothing. It is so dark," he could hear himself saying. "I must awake. The covenant! I must understand this covenant, and my responsibilities."

Suddenly there appeared before his eyes the vision of a smoking pot and a torch.

"The torch. I must grasp the torch. I must seal my end of this agreement."

Of itself, the torch began to move, passing between the split carcasses of the three dead animals.

"Lord, you have passed from your side to mine. Now a torch . . . I must have a torch. I must pass from my side to yours."

Once again the torch began to move, this time from the opposite end.

"Lord, you cannot do that! Will you hold up both ends of the covenant?"

Abraham!

"Yes, Lord."

> *You cannot be responsible*
> *for any part of this covenant.*
> *I and I alone am responsible*
> *for the keeping of the covenant*
> *between us.*
> *That which is my responsibility*
> *is mine,*
> *and that which is your responsibility*
> *is also mine.*
> *It is an everlasting covenant,*
> *established forever,*
> *by an indestructible, everlasting Life!*
> *My Life!*
> *Now hear my words:*
> *You shall live in this land,*
> *and so shall your descendants.*

> *There will come a day*
> *when your descendants will go into Egypt*
> *and there be made slaves.*
> *After four hundred years*
> *they shall return to repossess this land.*

"Lord, how shall I be the father of many nations? I have no children," came Abraham's struggling words.

> *You shall have a child from Sarah.*

"But she is barren."

> *Sarah shall bear a child.*
> *Now come. Behold the skies.*

Abraham fought to break loose from his sleep. "Am I mad? Or is this a vision of God? A vision . . . I have seen a vision!" he exclaimed, as he staggered out of his tent and into the night.

> *Do you see the heavens, Abraham?*

"Yes, Lord. I see. And I hear you! Clearly!"

> *Count the stars.*

"Yes, Lord. Oh, no. No, Lord, I cannot. They are too many to number."

Your descendants shall be as are the stars.

"Lord, can you be speaking of my loins? They are dead. Are you speaking of one of my kinsmen?"

> *No, I speak of you,*
> *of your wife Sarah,*
> *and your own children.*
> *Sarah shall bear a child,*
> *and that child shall be your heir.*

Abraham considered his loins. "Lord, that which gives life in me has long since died. And that which gives life in my wife—her womb also is dead and has been dead for a long time."

> *Do you believe*
> *what I have declared to you,*
> *Abraham?*

"Lord, I believe! I believe you can make my wife's womb alive. Lord, I believe you can resurrect my loins. I believe you can raise to life that which is dead!"

There was evident joy in the Lord's voice as he responded to Abraham's declaration.

> *You have believed,*
> *and in my eyes*

you are now right with me in every way.
In my eyes
you are holy.

The golden pen of Recorder, which had from the dawn of creation moved faster than light, almost slipped from the hand of this faithful angel. Taking a firm grip on himself, Recorder made entry into the Book of Records a most unbelievable statement.

Since the Great Tragedy, the fall of man, all men have done every imaginable thing to win God's favor, everything they could do to make themselves right with God. All have failed. But here is a man who has been found right in God's sight simply by believing that God will raise his loins from the dead. And for this . . . for this . . . God has counted this man to be righteous and holy!

Furiously Recorder continued.

How counter to all the ways and thoughts of man, and even to the thoughts of angels!

CHAPTER
Nine

"See how beautiful he is, my husband," said Sarah, beaming as she handed her firstborn to Abraham.

"Very beautiful, considering his father is a hundred years old, and his wife, ninety," replied Abraham with a gleeful laugh.

The proud parents of Isaac were certain their son would grow up in safety, marry, and have many children, thus fulfilling God's words to them. But such was not to be.

Abraham could not have been more shocked than on the day nearly a score of years later when God spoke to him concerning his only son in this land of Beersheba.

> *Go, Abraham,*
> *to Mount Moriah.*
> *Take your only son.*
> *Upon that mount*
> *sacrifice him.*

Abraham had to question his own ears.

"Lord, surely I have not heard you correctly. You would have me drive a knife into the heart of my son?"

"Take your son to Mount Moriah and there sacrifice him."

"But Lord, you have promised that from his seed would come a nation and . . ."

"Take your only son three days' journey to Mount Moriah. There sacrifice him upon an altar."

Brokenhearted, grieving, and half out of his mind, Abraham called two of his servants and his only son to go to a place in the north, not far from where Abraham had met the Priest of Salem.

Throughout the trek Isaac's eyes often focused on his father. What he saw was a troubled man who neither slept nor ate. Isaac too became filled with foreboding.

As the sun dawned on the third day of the journey, God called Adorae and Rathel to join him at the Door between the two realms.

"I have asked Abraham to do what I have asked no other man to do, and what no man shall be asked hereafter. Go, for it is the *third* day. See that no harm is done. But as man counts time, wait until the last possible moment to spare the life of this man's only son."

With those words, the Door between the two realms moved and then opened. Two angels stepped out into a dense forest just a short distance from the crest of Mount Moriah.

"Whatever it is that causes danger to this man or his son, I shall intervene," asserted Adorae. "Guard this place that no created thing interferes with Abraham."

"While you stand as their protector, I shall stand as yours," agreed Rathel. "They come. Be quick to move, for you will have only an instant to fulfill the Lord's word," Rathel continued.

"Draw your sword, Rathel. Thwart anything that comes this way, be it seen or unseen."

All morning long Abraham had searched to his right and to his left, hoping to see evidence of some divine deliverance, even as Mount Moriah grew unrelentingly closer. Every step Abraham took toward the mountain came with greater effort than the one before.

Abraham stopped. *I cannot do this,* he silently cried.

"Where is the lamb, father?" interrupted Isaac, speaking with total innocence.

Abraham could not answer.

Lord, it is the third day. My only son . . . Lord, will not the third day see his deliverance?

One last time Abraham looked to the heavens. Once more . . . only silence. No angel was to be seen. No God was to be heard. And the only sacrifice present was his son.

In what form could deliverance possibly come? Abraham wondered. *Isaac must bring forth a nation. Yet he stands before me as good as dead. Lord, do your words mean nothing? Or have I misunderstood? No, that is impossible. What then?*

In that instant Abraham found his answer.

There can be only one way out! I will slay my son. But God will raise him from the dead! That is it! God shall resurrect my son from the dead after he has been slain upon the altar of Mount Moriah.

Instantly, Abraham found his voice. "Isaac, you will go with me to the top of this mountain."

Turning to his two servants, Abraham continued. "Remain here. My son and I will make a sacrifice. When we have finished the sacrifice, we both shall return. *Both of us!* I repeat, soon I and *my only son* shall return to this very place.

"Isaac, come with me."

Father and son trudged up the hill.

"Father, where is the lamb?"

"Son, I believe you know. God himself will provide it."

The father built an altar, bound his son's hands and feet, and laid him gently upon the altar. With terror on his face but obedience in his heart, the son did not move. He uttered not a word, but only clenched his eyes and his teeth.

Abraham pulled forth from his garments a sharp blade, raised it high above his head, every sinew in his arms quivering with might and fear.

"My Lord and my God, now raise my child from the dead! I believe in the resurrection of my *seed!*" Abraham plunged the knife toward his son's chest.

The blade, glistening in the sun, drove toward Isaac's heart. Even as it closed upon his garment, a hand of awesome power reached out and caught the blade.

Adorae had done his job.

For an instant Abraham found himself trying to push the blade forward. Realizing the insanity of his action, he cried out, "No!"

And as he did, he heard the Lord's voice.

Stay your hand!

"My son, my only son!" Abraham, at the edge of sanity, threw the knife into a thicket and fell across Isaac's form. As Abraham untied the knots, Isaac opened his eyes and burst into tears.

There was a noise in the thicket. Father and son saw it at the same moment—a ram, its horns caught in the underbrush. In a moment they were upon the ram, bringing it and the recovered knife to the altar. There they sacrificed Isaac's substitute.

This done, Abraham began shaking all over. Soon he was sitting on the ground, convulsing in tears of joy. Father and son clasped one another furiously and rolled in the dirt, embracing, crying, their bodies shaking in unison, speaking words of comfort interspersed with sobs.

But in the other realm, the recording angel was the most troubled creature in all creation. He, too, was on the verge of tears, but for a much different reason.

"When the ram was slain, I heard a cry," groaned Recorder. "Even as the knife plunged into the ram's heart, I heard the faint echo of another cry. It was the echo of the piercing cry of a lamb, slain.

"I never realized until now . . . when I heard the ram's cry . . . it awakened a memory. Just as I was being created I heard *that* cry! At the very moment of my creation I heard it, the last reverberations, the echo of a distant wail. It was . . . it was the dying echo of the cry of a dying lamb.

"I have been blind! Nay, deaf! Why have I not remembered until now? Wait! There was another time I heard that cry. Yes. I remember now. I have heard it twice! That same awful wail . . . I heard it just as my Lord slew an animal to cover the nakedness of Adam."

Recorder was shaking all over. The recollection of these things never remembered was too much to bear.

"Thrice now I have heard that mournful cry. Nor did its sound come from earth. Nor heaven. Nor eternity! Its origin is before . . . and above, and beyond . . . outside . . . creation.

"But I must not place these thoughts into the Book of Records. None must know what even I have not remembered until now." With trembling hands Recorder wrote upon a tearstained page the following words.

Abraham believed in the resurrection, and God counted it to him as righteousness. A ram was slain. And a son, an only son, returned to his father. On the third day.

If another angel had been watching, he might have heard Recorder whisper these strange words.

That cry . . .
'tis the awful cry of a lamb
slain!
Before creation
slain!
Its echo reverberates
across creation
through the vaults of
eternity
and the corridors of
time.
O my God,
I cannot bear its sound.
But most of all
I fear
one terrible day
that which is
hidden somewhere
in times before the eternals
will intersect
with time
and become an event
in earth's history.

CHAPTER
Ten

Isaac grew into manhood and married a girl named Rebekah. She conceived twins. In her womb they fought. As children the twins fought. As young men they fought.

The older of the twins was Esau; the younger, Jacob. The younger lived for but one purpose—to supplant his older brother.

Jacob seized an opportunity to take his brother's birthright. His success only increased the enmity between the two. Later—when Jacob deceived his father and received the blessing due to his older brother—Esau in turn vowed vengeance, swearing he would kill Jacob. No one doubted his words.

Prompted by his mother, Jacob in fear took flight, leaving behind not only his family but the family's vast wealth.

Fleeing Canaan for the city of Haran, the fugitive Jacob came, late one night, to a lonely place called Luz. As he lay down to rest, his only shelter was the sky, and his pillow was a small stone. Staring up into the starry sky, Jacob had no greater thoughts in his mind than what was always there, deception.

And as Jacob wandered off into sleep, the Lord called a host of angels to meet him at the Door.

"The man you see lying there has within him the *seed* that will one day marry heaven and earth, making them one *again*," pronounced the Lord.

"A seed that can reunite heaven and earth, Lord?" queried Michael, giving words to the question in every angel's spirit.

"The seed," replied the Lord, "that is within his loins will one day cause. . . ." The Lord paused. His half-finished answer now became a question. "The two realms have not been one since Adam and the garden. Is there any creature who can cause them to join?"

"None, Lord," responded Gabriel.

The Lord turned again to Michael. "Is there any in heaven or earth who can cause these two realms again to be joined?"

Michael understood better than others that the Lord was about to reveal something of which angels had no previous knowledge.

"No, my Lord, none."

"Remain here."

With those words, the Lord stepped onto the threshold of the Door. In that moment Jacob awoke and looked into the sky and then blinked, not daring to believe what he saw. Eyes from both realms were now staring at the One who stood in the Door.

The Lord moved into the space between the two realms. He reached out and began drawing the two creations together. Closer and closer the two realms came to one another, yet they did not quite touch. But they were joined! The Lord himself held both of them, becoming a bridge that spanned the gulf between the two creations. *He* had become the joining.

Jacob rubbed his eyes. Stars shone forth against a canopy of dark blue, and in the midst of the sparkling blue sky . . . a hole.

"I see a Door. A magnificent Door. Opened. Beyond the Door, I see the glories of heaven. And in the heavenlies, angels! Angels as far as my eyes can see. Their light shines brighter than the brightest sun. And beyond them . . . *the throne of God!*

"But what is that . . . that which stands between me and the Door?" Jacob sat up. He wanted to rise and rush toward the opening, but he could find no strength to move.

"Is this a dream?

"This is no dream!

"There is heaven. Here is earth! The two are bridged. What joins them? I cannot see for the greatness of its light. A bridge? A ladder? No!"

For a moment it seemed Jacob could see a man. He closed his eyes, then opened them again.

"Great thunder! An angel has stepped out of the doorway.

"It . . . he . . . well, whatever it is . . . is using the

bridge . . . the ladder . . . or whatever it is . . . to come to earth."

Suddenly another angel passed through the Door onto the bridge and then onto the soil of earth.

"It must be a ladder that is allowing them to come here. But for a moment, through the brightness, I thought it was a man!"

Shimmering angels were pouring out of heaven, coming down some kind of steps and then boldly walking among the rocks and sand of Palestine!

A whole band of these aliens began moving toward Jacob. As frightened as he was, his eyes darted beyond them, for behind the angel he saw a magnificent person standing in the portal.

I am the Lord.
Your father, Isaac,
knew me as God.
Your grandfather, Abraham,
knew me as God.

Jacob began to shake all over. *Were my fathers so frightened when God spoke to them?* he wondered.

Now, Jacob,
know that the very land upon which you sit
shall I give to you
and to your descendants.
There will be as many of your children
as there is dust on earth.

Through your seed
shall all the families of earth be blessed.
I am with you
and will keep you wherever you go.
You flee in fear of your brother,
but one day I will bring you back to this land.
I will not forsake you
but will do what I have promised.

Jacob closed his eyes and then opened them again to assure himself of his sanity. He looked again toward the Door. Something of the very being of the One who had spoken to him was pouring forth out of him and cascading through the open Door. Whatever this sparkling cascade of light was, as it passed through the Door it seemed to change.

Again, Jacob strained his eyes in hopes of understanding what he was seeing.

"Angels on earth? A ladder? Something pours forth out of the being of God, changing as it reaches earth?"

As if in reply to his questions, the angels turned and began to ascend the mysterious ladder. In an instant they had returned to the heavenly realm. For a moment the ladder still joined earth to heaven, but only for a moment. Just for an instant, as the ladder disappeared, Jacob again saw the form of a man.

"The ladder is gone! The Door is closing.

"Wait!" cried Jacob.

From somewhere the words came again.

I will be with you.

At that moment, Jacob stumbled over something on the ground.

CHAPTER
Eleven

Jacob lumbered to his feet, wildly rubbing his fingers through his hair, trying to make sure he was awake.

"What did I see? Angels! I have heard my father speak of them. And God . . . did I see God? My father spoke of him. And the stories of my grandfather meeting the Lord of heaven and earth! This night did I see him? Yes. I saw him. And I saw glory.

"And . . . and he renewed his promise. To *me!* The land. My descendants . . . innumerable! My seed . . . it will bless all nations.

"What am I supposed to do?" cried Jacob to the skies. "Abraham! Isaac! What do I do?" he yelled frantically.

"Ah! My father built an altar. So will I. I must build an altar to the God who was *here.* For one bright moment God dwelt on earth! Right here. The Door to heaven was here too. And angels were here."

A half deranged Jacob began to cast wildly about for stones. While doing so his eyes caught sight of what he had stumbled over a moment before. He stooped down and picked up a small vase. He broke off the top.

"Oil!

"Is this something left by some stranger? Or did the angels bring it here, to me, from heaven?"

Jacob raised the vase above his head. "Something of heaven has been brought to this place."

Bending down, Jacob placed his hands on the stone that had been his pillow.

"Yes, a stone made of earth! Oil from the heavenlies! Something from both realms. I now make them one!" cried Jacob as he poured out the oil and smoothed it over the stone.

"Something of heaven . . . something of earth . . . one," he continued to mutter.

"This place shall be called the house of God, for God made his home here. And he gave me the promise of my forefathers."

Jacob faced in the direction where, shortly before, the Door to the heavenlies had opened.

"You have come to me as you have come to my fathers. You have given me the promise of this land and of my seed. But I am not content with this, for I am not my father nor my grandfather. I am Jacob. I am poor. I am alone. I am forsaken. I want you to bless me."

Jacob felt suddenly embarrassed by his words. Raising his head again, he tried what he concluded might be a better approach.

I thank you,
O Faithful One,
for kindnesses seen

and faithfulness shown.
You, God of heaven,
have stood upon this fallen earth.
You dared promise this land to me
and my descendants
forever!
Truly you rule the heavens,
and you are Lord of earth.
Therefore protect me
that these things may come to pass.
And do not forget to bless me!

As Recorder inscribed the words of this odd prayer, he could not help but remember the tragic day long past when Lucifer had claimed this earth and declared himself to be god of this planet.

"Perhaps Lucifer was a little hasty in his claims," whispered Recorder as a soft smile broke across his face. "Perhaps earth will once more be God's . . . indisputably . . . and heaven and earth will once more be one!"

While Recorder penned his words, Gabriel, who had been among the angels that descended to earth by way of the ladder, was inquiring of his God concerning these enigmatic events.

"Lord, what we have seen—does it foretell some future thing?"

The answer was less enlightening than it was confusing, causing Gabriel to wonder if he might have been better off had he not asked at all.

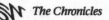

"You have seen heaven and earth joined by me."

"Yes, Lord. And what might it mean?"

"The *seed* of Jacob."

With those words, the Lord returned to the throne.

CHAPTER
Twelve

Jacob fled to the land of Haran and to his grand-father's kin, hoping to make a new start in life. He made his home in the house of Laban, brother of his mother, Rebekah.

Yet his new start was really not new at all. A conniver, a cheater, he always did things in an underhanded way. As to any changes in his character, his encounter with the Living God seemed to have been for nought.

But God is patient and sometimes also quite ruthless, as in the day when Jacob made such a mess of his life in Haran that he was once more forced to flee.

Caught between two men who swore vengeance on him, Jacob wondered if he might stand a better chance, after the passing of so many years, surviving his brother's wrath.

The answer came when news reached Jacob that his brother Esau was on his way to meet him, and in his company, four hundred men! No man needed four hundred men to help him greet his next of kin. Death at Esau's hands now appeared a certainty.

For the first time in his life Jacob fell on his knees in genuine contrition. But even as he prayed, his words had the unmistakable tinge of a man who found it quite difficult to be straightforward.

As Jacob clasped his hands together and pushed his knees into the dirt, he knew the only possible hope he had was in this God he hardly knew. Closing his eyes and bowing his head, Jacob made an effort at prayer.

O God of my fathers,
I am unworthy of
all your kindness.
I had nothing when
I fled Esau.
Yet now I have twice more
than I could have imagined.
O Lord, one more thing
I ask.
My brother, Esau . . .
I fear him.
Remember, you promised me
the promises of my fathers.
Therefore you have to save
me, O God,
from my brother's wrath.

His legs stiff, his face tearstained, Jacob rose to his feet. As he opened his eyes, he jerked back. A man was standing in front of him.

"Who are you, and from whence have you come?"
There was no answer, but in the eyes of this strange
creature, Jacob saw a dare. Almost in reproach, Jacob
addressed the man again.

"You gave a promise to my grandfather! You sealed
that promise with circumcision. You gave a promise to
my father, and you even *appeared* to him. They *walked*
with you. I hardly know you; nonetheless, that promise is for me too! You promised this land to me . . . and
to my descendants too. You said so! My seed will bless
the world, whatever that means. You promised me
that! And do not forget it either. Yet, even now, my
brother is on his way to kill me. Listen to me! I will not
leave this place until you treat me the way you treated
my fathers! Give me all that is rightfully mine."

Such audacity had rarely been seen by those in-
habiting the invisible realm. But even this audacity
paled in comparison to what next occurred. Jacob
lunged straight at the One who stood before him. As
he hit the stranger full on, Jacob cried again, "You
will not leave this place until I have received what is
mine."

A moment later Jacob realized he had chosen the
wrong approach. He was outmatched in both
strength and skill. Nonetheless, his adversary proved
to be tolerant, holding in reserve his overpowering
strength, allowing himself to exert no more strength
than that which Jacob possessed.

Muscle and sinew of each man challenged the
strength of the other. Thrown to the ground repeat-

edly, Jacob was instantly back on his feet, soon throwing his adversary to the ground. Each parried and lunged. At times their arms and hands locked for hours, neither willing to yield, yet neither overcoming.

As the night wore on, Jacob weakened, but his adversary, willingly or unwillingly, seemed to weaken also.

The battle continued on until the first rays of the sun painted the horizon and captured the silhouette of two strong men locked in an agonizing duel of will and strength.

Suddenly, Jacob's nameless foe stood erect and effortlessly threw Jacob to the ground. Jacob rose, only to be thrown again. This continued until every muscle in Jacob's body screamed with pain.

Feeling he could not possibly survive another tumbling, Jacob slowly rolled over in the sand and then lay very still. Unnerved, he looked about for his adversary. Instead, he saw the Door. The strange man was about to disappear through it.

That Door. He is going to go through the Door. I will never see him again. Never!

Staggering to his feet, and gritting his teeth to mask his pain, Jacob screamed, "No!" One last time he lunged at his silent foe, grappling him around the waist.

"You will not leave this place until you have blessed me," bellowed Jacob, as he threw the alien to

the ground. "Now tell me! What is your name? Who
... who are you?"

There was no answer. Jacob tightened his grip.

"Hear me! You will not leave this place until you are
not only the God of Abraham and Isaac, but also the
God of Jacob. Now bless me. Do you hear, bless me!"

In that moment Jacob discovered that in matters
such as this, the ways of God are not like the ways of
men.

"Your hip is the strongest part of you, Jacob."

"What?"

With those words the Lord threw Jacob to the
ground. "Your hip. It is the strongest part of you.
Now I will bless you."

The Lord lightly touched Jacob's hip. It shattered.
Jacob howled in pain.

"What have you done? You broke my hip. You
broke my hip! I cannot walk anymore. I am a cripple.
You have cursed me. Do you hear me? You have
broken my body. I am a weakling. I will be an
invalid. You have broken my . . ."

Jacob's voice trailed off as he stared wildly at his
useless hip. His next words were in a hoarse whisper.
"You did not bless me, just now, did you? If so, I have
been a fool to ask for *your* blessing! You have caused
me to lose all my stre—"

Jacob looked up. There was a faintly detectable
smile on the face of the victor. The wondrous One
knelt beside Jacob.

What is your name?

"Jacob!" replied the son of Isaac and grandson of Abraham, between sobs.

> *From this day forth*
> *your name is no longer Jacob.*
> *Prince of God*
> *are you.*
> *From your seed*
> *a seed shall come.*
> *By him*
> *shall all families of the earth*
> *be blessed.*
> *Now, Israel, arise!*

With these words, the man rose and disappeared through the Door.

Jacob pulled himself up. He could move only by limping. Every step was pain. "I have been blessed by God? I believe I have!"

From that day forward Jacob was a cripple, but he was a changed cripple. His duplicity had finally been driven from him.

And in his old age, Jacob—now Israel, sometimes called Prince of God—was found to be a man at peace with himself and the God in whom he trusted.

CHAPTER
Thirteen

The old man allowed his eyes to wander across the horizon—first to the north, then to the south, east, and west.

"There is not a cloud anywhere."

The land around Hebron was blistered and cracked. Israel could not remember the last time it had rained. Water was low. Food nearly gone.

"We will die here," sighed the Prince of God. "Unless my sons found help in Egypt, and unless they return shortly, we all will soon perish."

But his words, spoken to no one in particular, were not the center of his concerns. It was what his grandfather had once said that haunted him. "Your descendants shall go down into Egypt, and there they will remain for four hundred years."

"From childhood I heard the story: The sons of Abraham will one day move to Egypt. But never have I paid attention to it, for I never dreamed such an event might take place in *my* lifetime. Yet even now my sons *are* in Egypt.

"If they return to me safely, and if Benjamin is

with them, shall I allow all my family to move to Egypt? There—possibly—to stay four hundred years? Four hundred years is a *long* time."

The old man chuckled. "Unless my sons return soon, I will not have to be troubled with this matter. I will be dead."

"Master!

"Master, they are coming. You can see them in the distance."

"No, I cannot see them! I can hardly see beyond my nose," replied Israel, chuckling again.

In a few moments one of his sons emerged from out of the distant dust. Israel needed not to be told which son it was, for the man stood taller and broader than any other.

"Judah!"

"Father. We must all return to Egypt. Even you. We have been welcomed there."

"Benjamin? Is he safe?"

"Yes, Father, but there is more to tell."

"I am not interested. Tell me of Benjamin."

"We have returned with Benjamin."

"That alone suffices."

"Father, there is other news that will make you rejoice as greatly."

"There is no such news. If you speak of Egypt . . ."

"No, father, I speak of Joseph."

"Joseph! Have you found his body?"

"Father, your son Joseph is alive. And he rules all Egypt."

Quickly Judah reached out and grabbed his father, who was crumbling to the ground.

"It is not true . . . it cannot be true!"

"It is true, Father. Joseph is alive and he rules Egypt. There is none greater than he, save Pharaoh himself. And Pharaoh has invited *you* to live out your days in the safety and prosperity of Egypt."

"Judah, if we go, we will not return," replied the ancient one, drawing his eldest son closer to him. "I will die there, and so will you and your children. But your descendants will come back. Your great-grandfather, he prophesied that someday our future kin would return home."

Israel drew himself up, turned, and faced the skies, raising one hand as he did.

"Oh, my Lord, if I only knew for certain that this was the time and that it pleases you that we go into such a place as Egypt."

That night, as the old patriarch fell asleep, the Door opened once more. The Lord of heaven and earth stepped forth to speak to Jacob for the last time.

> *Israel, be at peace.*
> *Go down to Egypt.*
> *While you are there*
> *I will be there.*
> *One day I will indeed*
> *bring back your descendants.*
> *And while they sojourn in Egypt*
> *I will make of them a great nation.*

The next morning, the old man, his heart at peace, began preparation to move his family, his servants, his livestock, and all his possessions to a land known as Egypt.

And it was there that Jacob lived out his days. His people embalmed his body so that it might one day be carried home.

Jacob's sons and grandsons also died in Egypt. So also the pharaoh who knew and loved Joseph.

Eventually there arose a new pharaoh who knew nothing of Joseph. To this pharaoh these strange-looking people from Canaan, with their irrational culture and a religion that had but one god, were no more than his chattel. He owed these people nothing—neither time, interest, nor compassion. An iron fist holding iron fetters fell upon the descendants of Jacob; all were thrown into slavery. With each successive generation the lot of the Hebrews grew more grim. They came to be seen as the lowest of all humans in all of Egypt.

Each generation passed on to the next its poverty, its squalid huts, its chains.

And in all those long, wearisome years, not once did the Door between heaven and earth open.

The final ignominy came four hundred years later when Egyptian soldiers began putting the children of these slaves to death. But by the accident of man and the sovereignty of God, one of those children survived and was adopted into the house of Pharaoh. He grew up in the palaces of Egypt; but after committing a poorly concealed murder, he fled from Egypt's soil, becoming a fugitive in the most barren wasteland upon the face of the earth.

At the age of eighty years, this same man, now a herder of sheep—Moses by name—met his Lord at a burning bush.

Moses,
return to Egypt.
Free my people
and lead them back to Canaan.

Moses faced only one problem. Pharaoh was very much opposed to this idea . . . so opposed, in fact, that he endured plague after plague sent by God. Still Pharaoh would not yield either to Moses or his God. After all, the loss of all this manpower would destroy the very engine of Egypt's economy.

Yet if Pharaoh was opposed to the release of the Hebrews, so Moses was committed to carrying out God's command.

The tenth plague would end this test of wills.

PART

II

CHAPTER
Fourteen

"Nine plagues have fallen on this land, and nine times you have claimed that this god of yours is responsible. I do not believe it, and I will not let my slaves go. Call them the people of God if you wish, but I call them *mine.*"

"Then hear these words, Pharaoh," retorted Moses. "Thus says the Lord: 'Jacob is my firstborn. Let Israel go, or I will kill *your* firstborn.'"

Pharaoh was enraged. "Another plague? I believe in your tenth plague the way I believed in your first nine. My slaves will not depart!"

That day Moses walked out of Pharaoh's court for the last time. Returning to the Hebrew quarters of the city, Moses took his first step toward a massive flight of slaves from Egypt.

"Call the elders together, Aaron. Have Joshua help you. Gather them here, quickly. There is much to be done and little time for the doing."

While messengers spread out across the land to inform the elders of Israel of a meeting, another meeting, much larger, was being called by the Living God.

Congregating in two circling bands that virtually engulfed the throne, ten thousand times ten thousand angels swept around their Lord.

"This night the Door will open. Every citizen of the heavenlies will pass through the Door and visit earth. Take your place round about the treasure city of Pharaoh. But hold this foremost in your spirits: tonight you are not messengers, but *witnesses!* Take no action. But, rather, watch. And what you see this night, remember forever."

"How unusual!" whispered Adorae. "Have we ever heard such words?"

"I think not," replied Rathel. "And though I am glad, my spirit is, for reasons I cannot explain, quite uncomfortable."

"Your purpose on earth this night is but one: to learn to stand even while your whole being cries out to charge and destroy the enemies of God. Therefore sheath your swords. Only watch."

The Lord's words were followed by an almost unnerving silence.

"Do not pass through the Door until you hear the bleating of lambs rising up from the earth."

"The bleating of lambs—why?" was every angel's question.

"This night will I send Azell to visit every family in Egypt. Every firstborn of men and cattle will I destroy before the first rays of morning."

With the hearing of the name Azell, there came an angelic gasp.

"Do not seek to deter him. Seek not to save any from his domain. Only watch. Witness. And learn."

With those words, ten thousand times ten thousand silent angels lifted as one and swept toward the Door.

The throne room was once again occupied by but two beings, Recorder and his Lord.

"You will face him this night, will you not?" observed Recorder grimly.

"I will."

"And will I hear it again?"

For a long time the Lord stared at Recorder. Recorder stared back, neither blinking. A reply was unnecessary for the Book of Records, but one was needed for Recorder.

"Yes, you will hear it *again,* and Death shall be allowed to hear it for the *first* time."

"He does not know?"

"No. He could not know."

After a moment of silence, the Lord continued. "But this night he shall hear it and he will know. So also the host of heaven."

Recorder's eyes filled with tears. "I have heard that cry thrice now, my Lord. Oh, my God, must I hear it yet again?"

"One day, Recorder, you will not only hear but you shall see . . . the lamb . . . slain."

CHAPTER
Fifteen

All seventy of the elders of Israel were packed into the room, Moses in their midst. Faces taut, eyes grim and filled with fear—all awaited his words and their fate.

"Our Lord has sent Pharaoh nine plagues, yet he has not obeyed our Lord. Pharaoh has also declared to me that if I return to his throne room, I will die. Nonetheless, the words I speak to you will reach his ears. *Before the sun rises again,* Pharaoh will know that the Lord has sent the tenth plague."

"A *tenth* plague?" groaned one of the elders.

"The *last* plague. And with this plague, Pharaoh will let us depart from this land. Tonight Death shall visit all the land of Egypt. He will come from the east, visiting every household—"

Moses was interrupted. It was Isbod, the eldest and most loved of Israel's leaders.

"You are telling us the angel of death . . . will visit every home in Egypt. Are you serious? And will God save his people?"

"Yes, God shall save his people. This night God shall be our salvation from the greatest of all plagues.

"Now listen to my instructions. Leave here and spread out across the land. Go to every tribe. Speak in every house. Tell all the sons of Israel: '*Find a lamb*. Bring that lamb to your house and sacrifice the lamb. Then roast the lamb.'"

"But why?" came a query.

"On this very evening, before Death begins his visitation, place the blood of the lamb on the frame of the door to your home. Stay in the house. Where there is the blood of a lamb, Death cannot enter.

"When Death has passed you, eat the lamb with your feet shod, ready to flee at the sound of the ram's horn. Also be ready to take with you all the silver and gold you can. Be prepared to walk out of the land of Egypt *this night*.

"On this night, eat the lamb . . . eat all of it. No meat is to be found in your home at daybreak. The lamb will provide you the strength to leave Egypt."

Isbod interrupted, something of a chuckle in his voice.

"Moses, are you mad? And are you *certain* that God will save his people?"

"Yes, God will save his people," replied Moses assuredly.

"When you eat the lamb, eat also unleavened bread. And bitter herbs. As you eat the bitter herbs, remember how bitter it has been to live in Egypt. By the strength found in the slain lamb and in the bread, and in your memories of the bitterness of slavery, depart Egypt!"

"How can the blood of a tiny lamb save us from the death angel?" asked Aaron.

"Find a male lamb. Each household. The lamb is to be a year-old male. Roast that lamb. Eat it. Put the blood upon the doorposts. This is the Lord's word, and this we will do. And God shall save his people."

"This means that thousands and thousands of lambs must be found?" It was Isbod once more.

"Find the needed lambs among our herds, and find them among the herds of the Egyptians, for tonight their hearts will turn toward you. But remember, the firstborn of every family of all men and all cattle will die this night. The only protection is that blood."

Isbod rose to his feet.

"Hundreds of thousands of slaves—walking out of here in the midst of swords and chariots, protected from Death by no more than lambs' blood. Then . . . then walking out into a treacherous desert being led by a madman who grew up in Pharaoh's house." A smile broke out upon the craggy, sun-blistered face of the congenial elder. "Sounds just like God. Yes sir, sounds just like God."

As the elders departed, Moses called out to Joshua.

"Watch over the night. Make sure all is as the Lord has commanded."

Joshua's eyes narrowed as he sought to grasp the propensity and gravity of his mission.

"I must first go to my home and to my wife, Cordinel. She is alone with our firstborn, but she is a capable woman. She can prepare for this night even while I fulfill my duties."

As Moses nodded his approval, Joshua made his way out into the narrow streets of the Hebrew ghetto, his head filled with one terrifying thought. *My house is the easternmost in the ghetto. When Death reaches the Hebrews, my door shall be the first to which he will come!*

I am the firstborn of Nun. I have but one child, a son. I must be in my house with him and with Cordinel. But there is so much I must do first. All Israel must be prepared!

Joshua threw open the door of his hovel. His wife was not there. Joshua whirled about and would have rushed into the city when Cordinel appeared at the door, the afternoon sunlight causing her scarlet hair to glisten like brass. With face pale and terror dancing in her eyes, Cordinel rushed into Joshua's arms.

"I have heard. All firstborn males shall die tonight. Death is coming. Oh, Joshua, will God save his people?"

Joshua reached down and enfolded Cordinel's hands. They were like ice.

"Your hands . . . so lovely . . . I have never known them to be so cold."

"Oh, Joshua, I am frightened. We have but one child. And you also are a firstborn. Will he die tonight? Will you?" Cordinel searched Joshua's face for reassurance.

"Will God save his people?" she asked again.

For a moment Joshua stared at Cordinel, trying to find words that would reassure her. Quietly, she repeated his name.

"Yes, Cordinel, God shall save his people. Now go and find a lamb, a year-old male. Find one at all cost. It must be slain. Keep some of the blood. Roast it. . . ."

"Yes, I know. I have heard the instructions. I have already found a lamb. I have the grain. I have been given bitter herbs by an Egyptian woman."

"Good. You are not only the fairest but also the most remarkable woman in Israel. Now I must go. Moses has given me charge of many things this day.

"But where is our son?"

"He is playing with a little Egyptian boy, a friend. Do not be troubled, he always returns home about this time."

Cordinel slipped her arms around her husband and held him tight. Once more he heard her pronounce his name, and once more he responded.

"Yes, God will save his people. Now stay in this house. Let no one come through that door save our son and me. This night Death shall walk these streets. Ours will be the first house among the Hebrews he will seek to enter. Do not forget the blood of the lamb."

CHAPTER
Sixteen

Feverishly Joshua made his way from one end of the city to the other, giving instructions to elders, which they, in turn, were to pass along to the Hebrews throughout the country.

By now tens of thousands of Hebrews had poured out into the pastoral lands, every one of them hunting for a lamb. Having found one, each returned to his home to prepare the lamb that would cause Death to pass his home.

As Joshua continued his duties, he could not forget the fear he saw in Cordinel's beautiful eyes, nor the icy coldness in her hands. "So unlike her. Yet none of us knows our Lord well. None can be sure of this night."

Joshua found himself whispering to his Lord. "God, save your people. Lord, you are our salvation."

As nightfall approached, Joshua, curious about the results of his people's search for lambs, climbed onto a high roof to scan the countryside. As far as his eyes could see, the fields of Egypt were covered with tens of thousands of men coming back into the city, each

holding a lamb in his arms. The fields, catching evening's last light, appeared covered with snow from the whiteness of the lambs.

"Never has the human eye seen such a sight," Joshua whispered. "As far as I can see, lambs being brought to slaughter."

At that moment Joshua's ears caught the sound of a soft, quiet cry rising from the fields. It came from all directions, encircling the city.

"The bleating of the lambs!" Joshua fought back the urge to cover his ears. Never had he heard a sound with such pathos.

"It could chill the heart of God."

And while Joshua watched and listened, so also did the heavens.

"The bleating of the lambs," cried Gabriel.

At that instant the Door opened, and heaven emptied of its citizens as they poured out onto the hills and valleys surrounding Pharaoh's city. If human eyes had seen these fierce warriors, they would have beheld the greatest gathering of angels earth had known since creation.

"What a strange task," intoned Rathel. "Only to watch, but not to interfere. Come, Adorae, for I sense our place is at the entranceway to the Hebrew ghetto. We shall be the first to see Azell when he enters their quarters."

"We are not to prevent him, Rathel," urged Adorae.

"I remember," replied Rathel, a bit frustrated.

"I know that you remember, Rathel. That is not what concerns me. What concerns me is your temper."

"It shall be held firmly in control," assured Rathel.

"Not likely," retorted Adorae.

Taking their place before the house of Joshua, Rathel and Adorae stood stonefaced, awaiting the appointed hour. As they waited, the ears of men and angels began hearing screams rising from the Egyptian sector of the city.

"Midnight. The horror has begun."

"Where is Joshua?" asked Rathel in alarm.

"He has not returned. Nor is there blood upon the doorframe," replied Adorae. "This night Joshua and his son shall surely die."

CHAPTER
Seventeen

"Joshua's door not covered with blood!" exclaimed Rathel, drawing his sword.

"Temper, Rathel! You are out of your spirit!" pleaded Adorae. "There is neither use nor purpose in drawing your sword against Azell."

"I know," replied Rathel, his eyes blazing with rage. "Nor is there any power in the universe allowed to stop him. But I . . ."

"It is Joshua!" cried Adorae.

Joshua threw open the door. Cordinel sat in a corner, frozen in terror.

"Our son . . . where is he?"

"He never returned. Oh, Joshua, I do not know where his playmate lives. I have searched everywhere. No one knows anything. I cannot find him. And the screams! Have you heard? They draw closer. Even now that *thing* comes our way."

Joshua wasted no time with an answer, but darted out into the fearful night, a firstborn seeking his firstborn.

"Azell!" cried Adorae.

A gurgling roar pierced the night. "Now to the children of God. I, Death, have come for you, contemptuous Hebrews. This night you belong to me." Raising his claws in the air, he cried again. "And *nothing* can stop me. Nothing."

Rathel, sword drawn, stepped straight into the path of Azell.

Azell looked down in disbelief, then howled in fiendish laughter.

"I fear you as I fear an insect!" bellowed Death. "Out of my way, puny messenger of your puny God."

Rathel did not move, but rather thrust forth his jaw. "I have a question for you, Azell."

"Fool, do not hinder my appointed hour."

"I have a question for you, Azell."

"Out of my way," cried the monstrosity.

"My question is this: Who can stop you?"

"None can stop me! There is none who can kill Death. How can Death die?" Azell's fiendish laugh shook the very ground on which Rathel stood. Azell's black eyes glistened with glee. "I am forever. I am the final conqueror, the last citizen of creation. And then even creation shall be drawn into me. So also will be your fate. Even the eternals will one day die in me!"

"But *if* you could die, *if* you could taste your own venom . . . how might such a thing come to pass?"

For an instant the bizarre question caused Death himself to wonder.

"There is no such means. None! It would take one who is my equal." His words now spewed from his vomitous mouth with hideous delight. "But there is none my equal," he roared with delight. "If there were such a one, he alone could bring me to my end; but in so doing, he also would die."

Azell laughed hideously, then cried again, "None! None! None!"

"Truly, you are a fiend, Azell," replied Rathel, sheathing his sword, but not before Joshua had bolted into his home, his son in his arms.

"You are a magnificent fool, Rathel," came the admiring words of Adorae.

"But are we too late?"

CHAPTER
Eighteen

"The blood, where is the blood?" cried an almost deranged Joshua.

Cordinel, her face swollen from tears and her voice frozen in fear, motioned toward the blood of the lamb.

Once more Joshua hurled himself through the door, recklessly splattering the blood *everywhere* until the doorposts, the header, the door, and the ground beneath were soaked with the dark red of a lamb's blood. Even as he rushed back inside, Joshua could feel the cold breath of Death on his neck.

Inside, Joshua enveloped Cordinel in his arms.

"Now is God our salvation," murmured Joshua. "Now is God our salvation."

But outside, Death had acknowledged the blood by no more than a contemptuous sneer.

CHAPTER
Nineteen

"What is this upon the door of one whose useless name is Joshua? The blood of a lamb? There is no salvation from God this night. The blood of a lamb? A slain lamb? There is nothing more unlikely to stop me or deliver Israel than the blood of a mere lamb!"

Azell threw back his head and cried to the heavens. "Hear this, you who are Life. This night I shall take *all*. Tonight I shall bring the seed of Jacob into *my* kingdom. Tonight his future seed is vanquished. Forever."

Every angel gasped at such audacity; they trembled in wonder yet disciplined their rage. "We dare not move, but only witness," said each angel, reaffirming his orders.

Azell lowered his head. Someone had stepped in front of him and blocked his way into Joshua's home. Seeing the face of the intruder, Death roared.

"You!"

We meet again, Azell.

"You dare come to earth! And in the form of man? Be warned, Life . . . *men* die. You would dare stand before this door. You cannot prevent me. No one can. You whom they call God shall *not* be salvation this night. You have failed!"

> *It is my earth, Death.*
> *Not yours.*

"Hear me. I am the sickle that harvests all things that live. Since the day of the fall until this hour . . . and on . . . and on until the end of all things, I *am* the final end of this creation. Now step aside, Life. You, better than any, know you cannot keep me from my prey."

The god of all dying looked into the face of the Lord of Life and spewed, "You will be entombed in me one day. I shall be your shroud and your coffin."

> *Shall Life be in Death?*

The Lord spoke with a voice unnervingly calm.

"Yes!" came Death's reply, spoken almost in ecstasy.

> *If Life shall be in Death,*
> *shall Life come out of Death?*

"Never!" screamed Death. "I would die before I would release you!"

The Lord smiled.

Yes, you would, Death.
Yes, you would.

"Enough of this senseless gibberish. Out of my way!"

With those contemptuous words ringing in angelic ears, the Lord placed his head against the lintel above the door and stretched out his hands upon each side of the door. As he did, blood began to pour from his face and hands.

"You are dying," cried Death, his voice reflecting his own terror. "From your hands and head . . . *your* blood. And your side, wounded! No! What is this that I see . . . that you, Life, are *slain!* That is not possible, for I know all dyings since the beginning of creation. There is no record of such a death."

At that moment, time stopped. Eternity ceased its trek. The figure standing before Death began to change. For an instant the eyes of Death thought he might have seen God become a lamb. Then, for an even briefer moment, he thought he saw beyond Joshua's door . . . a hill, a tree, a stake, a blood-soaked man . . . dead!

Recorder shut his eyes, gripping his pen with all his might, for he knew what would follow.

It began.

Somewhere from out there beyond creation, before time, before and above the eternals . . . a cry!

Creation had never heard or dreamed of such a piteous wail, one not unlike the sound of the bleating of a lamb at slaughter; yet the origin of the cry was from places unknown to either heaven or earth. It came from beyond the eternals, in the age before the ages, telling of an event that took place *in God* even before he set forth his creation.

"An event that belonged to no continuums, a slaying as inclusive as the All of God. Creation is wrapped inside that lamb. Slain . . . before . . . creation," sobbed Recorder.

"That wail—that awful wail! From whence does it come" cried Death.

For the first time ever, Death staggered back, lifting an arm in self-protection from the cry.

"What was it that cried?" Death asked, almost pitifully. "I know not its time nor place of origin. This dying is a thing unknown to me." His words were more a curse than an observation.

"A dying I know nothing of? That cannot be! I know every death this creation holds! From whence came those wounds that I beheld? I alone can slay! I saw *him,* dying, yet it was not my work; therefore, it cannot be. From whence, then, this wail of death?"

The hideous face of Death contorted in its first taste of fear.

Acting wholly on instinct, Recorder slammed down his pen, a thing he could do only when his Lord had halted time and eternity in their flowing. Having lost all presence of mind and breaking with

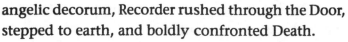

angelic decorum, Recorder rushed through the Door, stepped to earth, and boldly confronted Death.

"You know not all things, you beast!" raged Recorder. "Hear what *I* know. There is a dying you never knew occurred."

"Impossible," howled Death. "I—"

"Shut up and listen, craven one!" thundered Recorder. "You do *not* know all things, incarnate arrogance! There was One slain *before* creation!"

"No!" yelped Death, showing uncertainty for the first time ever.

"Yes! And I was witness to the wound. The echo of the cry of that death I heard even as the worlds were formed."

Without another word Recorder vanished, reappearing beside the throne. Reaching for his golden pen, time once more began to flow.

Defiantly, Death thought to push his way toward Joshua's door once more. But the blood of a Lamb, which no Hebrew had ever seen, nor Death had ever known, forbade him.

Death lifted his claws to the skies.

"You have stopped me this night. But, oh, the price! Have you stopped me with the blood of a dying that belongs outside creation? Ah, then, one day that dying must enter time. And when it does, I will be there! Then you will be held in my clutches . . . forever!"

Death swung about to search out his next victim. As he went from house to house, he screamed again.

"Your blood is on every door! Damn you, Life. I will not rest until you are mine."

Death stepped into the center of the street, calling out to the heavens one last time. "All things covered by your blood I pass over. But an hour comes when I will not pass over *you*, O Lamb, slain. Hear me, Life! *I* will be there waiting for the blade that strikes. One day—somewhere, somehow—this mysterious dying must intersect time. I await you there, my only foe!"

And from the heavens came the reply of him who is Lord of all.

> *I will be there, Death,*
> *awaiting you.*
> *And we shall not retreat*
> *until one is victor.*

"I will cover you with my wings, Life. Think not to destroy me, Life. For Death, being not alive, cannot die!"

> *You know not all things, Death.*
> *Your prey be man.*
> *Come for me*
> *when such I am.*
> *Then shall Death meet death*
> *and die.*
> *There will be no more dying then.*

Death sneered and turned to go.

"We must leave here, Rathel. The night is ended," Adorae spoke quietly.

"Yes," responded Rathel. "But, oh, what a night to remember!"

"Do you grasp all that we have seen?" continued Adorae, in words clothed with awe.

"No, but this I do know. Our Lord sent all the hosts of heaven to this place to prepare us for another night not unlike this one."

"It will be a dreadful night. I feel it already," replied a shivering Adorae.

Rathel's response to Adorae was not unlike Recorder's entry into the Book of Records.

This night is but a foretaste of one to come.

CHAPTER
Twenty

Joshua and Cordinel remained frozen in one another's arms, their eyes fixed on the door. The screams coming from the city had ceased, but was it safe to emerge?

"There have been no anguished cries from among the Hebrews, Joshua. Has the blood prevailed? Has Death passed us by?"

Joshua was about to venture an answer when someone rattled the door.

"Is it Death?" whispered Cordinel, her emerald eyes flashing panic.

Once more the door rattled vigorously.

"It has to be a human!" came Joshua's reply, taking his first full breath in hours.

"Are you in there, Joshua? Are you safe?"

"It is Moses!" exclaimed Cordinel.

Joshua unbolted and swung wide the door, as one making entrance for a king. There was a light in the eyes of Moses and almost a smile on his face!

"Throughout Pharaoh's city . . . we are not sure what has happened, but you have heard the cries.

Among us, not one firstborn has been lost. Not one! The blood prevailed!"

Hearing those words, Cordinel crumpled to the floor and began to weep quietly. But just then the eerie silence of early dawn was broken by the piercing sound of the ram's horn. Looking out, Joshua could see the streets beginning to fill with people.

Moses turned to Joshua. "You know the plan. I will lead the people out. You, Joshua, must be the very last."

Moses then addressed Cordinel. "Have you roasted a lamb?"

"I have," responded Cordinel.

"And have you eaten it?"

"No, not yet."

"Then eat the lamb and the bitter herbs. Do it in haste. The blood of a lamb has set us free, and its body shall be our strength to leave Egypt. Once we have departed this place, we will not cease our march until we have crossed the Red Sea and penetrated deep into the desert, so find your strength in the lamb.

"Now I must go. Joshua, a most unexpected thing . . . a number of Egyptians have chosen to go with us. Also, many of our people have been given gifts of gold and silver."

Moses then added with a quiet chuckle, "I am not sure the gifts were given out of benevolence. For some it was the gift of riddance."

With that, Moses walked to the door, but turned for a departing word. "No longer slaves!" he cried, raising one hand as he spoke.

Joshua, Cordinel, and their only son sat down in their tiny hovel for their final meal in Egypt. They knew they were to finish all of the food, yet several times Joshua determined he would not eat another bite. It was the bitter herbs that were so difficult to abide. As he chomped down on those pungent herbs, a lifetime of suffering passed before his inner eyes. And not only *his* sufferings, but the suffering and demeaning of his father, Nun, and all his ancestors before him. He recalled again the stories his father and his grandfather had told him of whippings, dishonor, and cruelties.

Joshua rose to his feet defiantly. "Four hundred years of abuse end today. The bitterness of Egypt will cease forever." With those words he swallowed the last sour herb.

"Cordinel, take our son. Go! You will find greater safety in going now with the others. I will find you somewhere on the journey."

Joshua threw open the door, revealing a street now flowing with refugees. Some carried sacks on their backs, others dragged their belongings behind them. Many, though, had nothing, not even shoes. A few were on horses, fewer still in wagons loaded down with household possessions, but most were on foot. Herds of goats and sheep pressed forward with the crowd.

The escape had begun!

Cordinel was about to join the sea of living humanity when Joshua reached out to her.

"Your face, once more." For a silent moment Joshua gazed down on Cordinel. "It is the loveliest face in all this world. I shall hold it in my memory until I meet you again."

Cordinel disappeared into the throng with their son. Joshua, in turn, moved in the opposite direction, pressing his way against the human tide.

"None must be left behind."

For hours Joshua combed streets and homes, calling out as he did. Finally he came to the end of the throng.

"Everyone seems to have departed," Joshua said to himself. At that moment several elders of Israel approached.

"Are there more?"

"Not to our knowledge," replied one elder.

"Yes, there are two. See! There!" replied another. "That old man and the boy with him. The old man refuses to come."

Joshua rushed down the street and knelt beside an ancient Israelite and a little boy.

"He is my great-grandson. We will not go."

"Why?"

"Because I am too old and he is too young."

"You prefer to be a slave in Egypt?"

For a moment the old man did not answer.

"Let me say this. I do not know the wilderness, and

I have never seen the land that was promised to our forefathers. But I *have* heard stories of the desert. The heat rises to twice that of the human body. Few have passed through that inferno and lived. And now Moses would take hundreds of thousands of us through it. No, I am too old."

"And what of the boy?"

"He will stay with me, for I am all he has."

"What has it been like for you here, old man?"

"It has been the madness of a nightmare," came the old man's hoarse reply.

Joshua stood up and looked around. A door to one of the now-empty dwellings stood open. Joshua rushed in, reappearing a moment later with a bowl in hand.

"Old man, have you eaten the bitter herbs?"

"No, for I am not going."

"Eat!"

"Why?"

"Do as I say. Eat!"

The old man bit down on the herbs. "Phew! This is too bitter for anyone to eat."

"Egypt is too bitter for you to stay."

The old man's teeth crunched down again. "This is terrible," he said, his face puckering as he spoke. He was about to spew it out when Joshua demanded, "No! Eat."

Joshua continued, "Have you ever been beaten?"

"Yes," replied the old man indignantly.

"But you have safety here?"

"*Hrumph!*" The old gentleman's face contorted with his next bite.

"Has your soul cried out for food?"

"Well . . ."

"And was your hunger satisfied?"

The old man looked up at Joshua, searching his face.

"No! Absolutely not."

"But you did have security in Egypt?"

"Yes, if you call leeks and garlic and a mat *security!*"

"Perhaps you are right, old man. Perhaps it is wise to stay with chains . . . and the known!"

The old man chewed in silence, pondering this odd conversation.

In a moment his eyes brightened. "Those chains! Look. Here! See the scars on my wrist. And the beatings. And the insults. Every time they spoke it, they bit off the word *Hebrew.* They ridiculed my God. They left me to make bricks with mud, not even with straw. And the food they gave us . . . it had much fat in it, yet it was not good for our bodies. And . . ."

The old man bit down on a particularly odious herb.

"But shall God be our salvation in the desert?"

"Was God our salvation this night?"

"Yes!" cried the old man. "God *is* our salvation!"

Looking at the little boy beside him, the ancient one reached down and inspected the unscarred wrist of the child, then gazed again at the scars on his own.

"The *security* of slavery is not worth the chains that go with it!" the old man exclaimed as he rose to his feet. "Better the hope in the unknown than *this* kind of damnable security. Egypt is not worth her security and slavery."

The old man turned to the little boy. "My son, we shall learn to walk on hot sand."

"Then you will go?"

The old man threw down the bitter herbs. "This day the bitterness of these riches has ended. Freedom in poverty and walking in the unknown has begun."

The old man straightened his shoulders, clasped the little boy's hand, took a few steps, and then broke into a run. "God has let his people go!" he cried. "And I will be one of them. And my great-grandson shall live in the land of promise!"

Joshua called out after him. "And may all your descendants come to know what you have learned!"

It was in that moment that Joshua caught sight of something in the corner of his eye. He turned to see what it was.

"A light . . . a strange light in the sky. Never have my eyes beheld a light such as this!"

CHAPTER
Twenty-One

The Lord stood at the Door watching the Israelites make their way through the streets of Raamses and out into the countryside.

"I shall lead them, for they do not know where they should go," said the Lord quietly.

The Door moved just ahead of the vast line of humanity that was forming below, the glow of heaven seeping out the Door.

Just a short distance below the light and the Door could be heard the voice of Moses.

"There, in the skies above us. Follow the light. The light of the Lord shall lead us out of Egypt."

"Recorder," called the Lord. "As you inscribe what you see, write also these words.

There shall come a day, in the fullness of time, when I shall be a pillar of fire by night and a cloud of fire by day to lead my people, but not as in this hour. At that time I shall be a fire that leads people, not in the sky above, but from within . . . in their spirits.

Once again came the voice of Moses.

"The pillar of fire. This is our God leading us out of Egypt's wealth and splendor and out of slavery. Forward, now, into his freedom."

The eyes of all Israel turned toward the fiery light billowing forth just above them.

"So beautiful," whispered Cordinel. "Never have I seen such glory. Never could I have imagined such beauty!"

"It is the glory of our Lord," came a voice from behind her. As Cordinel turned, she felt the strong arm of Joshua draw her to him.

"Joshua! God *is* our salvation. And he has set us free! Oh, Joshua, we have learned so much about our Lord this night. My heart is so assured!"

Ahead, the voice of Moses boomed again.

"The fire of God leads us in the darkness. And on it shall lead us into tomorrow and into tomorrow's night. But be quick. The heart of Pharaoh will turn. He will come to destroy us!"

Cordinel clasped the arm of her husband tightly, and, with tears that caused her emerald eyes to glisten, she once more whispered her husband's name. Then she added triumphantly, "And God shall be our salvation if Pharaoh comes!"

"*When* he comes," cautioned Joshua.

CHAPTER
Twenty-Two

The people of Israel came to the banks of the Red Sea. As they did, the pillar of fire stopped.

All Israel watched as the fire above them moved back across the host of Israel. In a moment the light was just above Israel's rear guard.

Suddenly the earth began to shake. Someone cried, "The chariots of Pharaoh!"

At that instant the pillar of fire plunged to earth, coming down just behind the last Israelite.

Between God's people and the army of destruction rested the fire of God. Six hundred of Pharaoh's mighty charioteers—followed by lesser chariots unnumbered, and beyond them swordsmen and foot soldiers as far as the eye could see—all came to a halt before the hindering fire of heaven. Nonetheless, an army that stretched out beyond the reaches of the human eye struck terror in the hearts of runaway slaves.

"Moses, we will perish—by water or by sword!" someone screamed. Soon the cry was taken up by

hundreds of thousands as men and women rent their garments and threw dust on their heads.

"Lord!" cried an astonished Moses. "Why? Lord, why has Israel cried out to *me?*"

"Tell them to move straight forward."

Moses clenched his jaw and moved straight toward the waters. An entire race, certain of its impending death, followed him. A wall of fire held the armies of Pharaoh at bay. But what of the waiting sea, hungry to swallow its prey?

Just then came the sound of a mighty wind rushing toward them from out of the east.

"Look. Beyond the sea, coming this way."

Like all the forces of heaven released at once came a torrent of wind, blistering the faces of the Israelites as it approached. "Save us, our God. From wind, water, and sword. Save!" rose thousands of voices.

The people watched as Moses raised his staff over the waters. Every eye knew that staff. It had confronted Pharaoh and his magicians. It had turned the mighty Nile to blood.

When the convulsing wind reached the sea, the begrudging waters parted under the pounding of its unseen powers. As the water parted, the howling wind turned the now-naked sands to dry powder.

The tornado of air continued moving across the sea until it created two giant walls of water.

"A mountain of suspended water to our right and to our left!" called Moses in breathless awe, his rod still outstretched over the sea.

"A path through the waters of death!" cried an exhilarated Joshua.

"Forward!" roared Moses.

And though few heard his voice, all understood. The descendants of Jacob poured across the banks into the narrow divide. Into the waters of death swarmed an entire race, the other side beckoning to them of a new life.

All Israel forged their way into the tiny path between towering walls of obedient water. Some went in carts, some on foot, and some were carried on strong shoulders. A number stopped and stared at the watery walls, a few children even daring to poke their finger into the churning waters, laughing with glee, then running on.

A few who entered that small strait between the walls of water fainted in terror. But as more and more reached the far bank, calling to those behind them to be of good courage, some actually began to shout. A few began to sing. Soon the chorus was joined by thousands, as a few hearty souls actually stopped and danced upon the floor of the sea. Jubilation swept Israel. From one end of the throng to the other, praises to God could be heard.

"Look!" exclaimed Cordinel, watching from the far side as the last of the host crossed over. "The coffin of Joseph!"

A cheer of glory rose up from a million voices. "Joseph is going home!"

Full-throated, the exslaves cried in cadence, "All

Israel is going home. Glory to God, Israel is going home!"

A song of thanksgiving ascended to the God of heaven as a people enslaved for four hundred years found again their tongues of praise.

Over six hundred thousand men trooped through this strange pathway to their freedom that day. With them came their wives, their children, and the booty of Egypt.

Just as the rays of the morning sun broke across the sands, the pillar of fire, hovering on Egypt's banks, lifted. Israel was unprotected.

"Forward," cried Pharaoh. "The gods of Egypt have made a way for the armies of Egypt to recapture their slaves. Slay those who resist!"

Egypt's armies rushed after the Hebrews, plunging bravely into the narrow path of dry sand, trusting that power belonged to their gods.

The chariots were the first to thunder in. It seemed they would soon reach Israel. Behind the chariots rushed thousands of soldiers, bellowing their war cry. But as the chariots reached the far side of the sea, some became stuck in a sand no longer dry.

Panic ensued as chariots overturned. Soldiers began to scream, "God is with these people. It is the Living God who fights for them and against us. Turn back!"

"Stretch out your staff once more, Moses," came the word of the Lord. Instantly Moses' hand went out toward the breach. The waters howled, convulsed, and collapsed in a horrendous roar. The earth shook under the feet of the Israelites as the gigantic walls of water crashed to the ground.

Egypt's warriors disappeared in the blink of an eye. Almost instantly the water found its level and resumed its calm, its prey hidden beneath its peace.

Israel stared out across the sea.

"Look! A chariot floating by."

"There, the body of one of the finest of Pharaoh's horses."

"And there—a man. Dead! And another. And yet another!"

"It seems that all of Egypt has been drowned in the sea. Egypt, plunged beneath the waters of destruction, is no more! Baptized into death. The world of Egypt has died to us. That world no longer exists. We are free of the Egyptians, by means of death."

"To them . . . we are dead, gone, nonexistent. To us . . . they are dead, gone, forever."

"*Death* set us free."

"We must go on. Let us find what awaits us in the wastelands."

Marching in stunned silence, Israel moved from the banks of the sea and out into the forbidding desert.

PART

III

CHAPTER
Twenty-Three

The great procession wound its way into the desert and came to a place that would come to be known as Mara. There the former slaves found water aplenty, but it was bitter and undrinkable.

"Food we have, but not water," said Moses as he considered just how many people there were in his charge who needed water. The thirsty throng stretched beyond the horizon. Every mouth waited as Moses cast about for a solution to this mounting crisis.

"There is water unlimited, yet undrinkable," he continued. "We have been delivered by God and a lamb. But unless we have water, we will not have life."

Slowly, thoughtfully, Moses walked to the headwaters of the vast Mara reservoir.

"Moses is coming this way, Lord," came the words of a surprised Recorder, for it was unusual for the Door to open at the very throne of God.

Moses raised his voice to the heavenlies and to God, not realizing his feet stood but a short distance from the throne, nor that the River of Life, gushing out of the midst of the throne, flowed nearby.

Moses waited, not knowing that his Lord was so near, nor that he was plucking a branch from the Tree of Life. In a moment the Lord cast the branch through the Door, landing—now visible—at Moses' feet.

Moses looked down.

"Where did that come from? It appeared out of nowhere."

Moses picked up the branch and examined it. "Too ordinary to be of God," he mused.

Yet, beyond intuition or understanding, Moses knew he was to cast the branch into the bitter water. And so he did. That day a million rejoicing souls drank of the sweetest water they had ever tasted. A lamb had given them deliverance and food. A tree had given them life.

Recorder, always sensing a higher drama and a deeper meaning, could not but make the following entry.

Is it really possible? Shall God one day return to earth the Tree of Life and the River of Life? To a fallen earth, covered with fallen men? Can such things be?

And as Recorder wrote, Moses sat upon the banks of Mara, looking out over the wasteland that lay before them, considering—perhaps for the first time—the grim realities that faced over a million people crossing a waterless, foodless subcontinent of sand.

"O Lord, how shall we cross this scorched void without dying of hunger and thirst? How will you provide for us?"

CHAPTER
Twenty-Four

All Israel slept. Sunrise was still hours away. There was but one lone figure to be seen making his way through the tiny spaces between the endless rows of tents.

As he walked, he heard a baby cry, an old man cough. Passing one particular tent, he heard the voice of a little boy. "Mama, I dreamed I saw God. I really did."

He smiled and continued on, his feet making no footprints in the loose sand.

A few moments later the stranger effortlessly climbed the side of a sand dune, turned, and surveyed the scene. Twinkling lights from oil lamps blinked before every tent.

"Israel, you feel very much alone, do you not, and frightened? Every day you raise your murmuring to my throne." He smiled faintly. "You do not understand me, and you wonder if I understand you. Tonight you are tired; tomorrow you will be hungry. Very soon you will once more exhaust your hoard of water. Food and drink are your constant need.

"Creatures of the spiritual realm also have the need of nourishment. As your bodies need nourishment, so also do spirits need food. Oh, Israel, in this very hour you have need of nourishment of which you know not. There is a spiritual realm that lies dormant within you, even now. You know so little of this truth, but one day your children will know. As I am the food of heaven, so shall I be the food of man and the spiritual food. And one day it shall come to pass that man will also drink of the spiritual water that will reside within his inmost being."

The Lord sighed a wearisome sigh. "Nonetheless, on the morrow I will meet the needs you *do* understand. As morning breaks I will give you bread.

"No, not real bread! But a shadow of what is real. A picture of *that day* when I will give you real bread. In that day I will give you bread not for your body, but for your spirit. I Am the bread you need the most. I Am *real* bread. What I give you tomorrow is but a shadow of myself."

With those words, the Lord rose up from the sand dune, ascending into the sky directly over the camp. In that moment he seemed to break apart into millions of pieces. These pieces, like sparkling diamonds falling from the sky, descended softly and came to rest upon the earth.

"I Am the bread from heavenly places."

The first rays of the sun caught the shiny white

objects that lay scattered about the ground, glistening in concert with the morning dew. The whole encampment was covered with this mysterious gift from realms spiritual.

CHAPTER
Twenty-Five

A young boy stuck his head out of a tent, yawned furiously, looked around, and then cried to one of his parents, "Mother, what is that?" Scratching his head, he continued, "Mama, come look."

"What is what?" she asked.

The boy cracked open the tent flap. She, too, looked out. Startled, she exclaimed, "What is it?" The father raised his head from his mat and caught a glimpse of the white-covered ground. "I do not know what it is," he said. Throwing the tent cover wide open, he stepped out into the morning light with his family, there to stare at a land covered with small flakes of . . . *something.*

"What is this?" he mumbled as he hurried out to pick up one of the pearl-like objects. Others were doing likewise. The whole camp soon scurried out onto the ground, picking up this strange stuff and addressing the same question to the food in their hands. Not knowing what to call it, they gave it the name *what-is-it.*

Whatever what-is-it was, it was cool, it was round,

it was white, it was juicy, it was tasty, something like honey. It was delicious. But most of all, it was *bread*.

But from where had this bread come? The skies had been clear all night—the watchmen testified to that. Men had never seen anything like it nor known anything to compare it to. Surely, all concluded, this was bread from the heavens.

"If this bread falls from the sky each morning," all agreed, "it will feed us through the wilderness!"

But Moses understood they had been but *half* rescued. Looking up into the sky, he addressed his anxiety to his God.

"The skies provided us with bread, but the skies out here do not rain water, Lord. Do you have ways of bringing us water?"

CHAPTER
Twenty-Six

Moses kicked the hot, dry sand beneath his feet. It was not like the dark, fertile soil of the Nile's delta. Earlier, near the Red Sea, there had been moisture in the light soil, but this was sand—white, hot, grainy, and dead—as far as the eye of man could see.

Waves of heat rose up from all directions. Everywhere Moses beheld dusty whirlwinds in their perpetual dance, and to the east he could see a killer sandstorm approaching.

"I have lived out here before," groaned Moses, heaving a hard sigh. "Every inch cries, 'There is no water.' Men can walk for days, even weeks, without seeing so much as a drop. What might it take to bring sufficient water to this people, surrounded by a sea of sand? And if we had a sufficient supply today, what of tomorrow, for we cannot drag with us enough water to supply our needs across this endless inferno.

"We do not have water. If we did, we could not carry it. Lord, are we doomed? It has been days since your people drank water. They are exhausted, dis-

couraged, and on the verge of mutiny. Yet the hardest part of this trek lies ahead of us. Lord, . . ."

Once more Moses kicked the hot sand, this time speaking to himself.

"If I have understood my Lord correctly, this day he will supply us with water. For today? But how will he find water for all our tomorrows?"

With those words spoken, Moses laboriously climbed a huge flint rock rising above the desert floor. Beyond, from the west, came that endless column of humanity moving toward him and the flint rock.

By noon the throng had become a crescent; by afternoon the human sea of Hebrews had almost encircled the mighty rock.

The cruel sun reached its vortex. Everyone was exhausted. Many could hardly stand; some fell prostrate into the sand. As were men, so also were the cattle, bellowing, bleating for just one thing: water for their parched throats.

But most pitiful of all were the cries of the children pulling at their parents' garments, begging for a drink, not able to understand why water did not come to mouths so dry.

The mound upon which Moses stood was the largest flint rock he, or anyone, had ever seen. A few of the elders climbed up on it to join Moses in this crucial hour.

Isbod spoke. "Water? Here? Moses! You are mad! You know that, do you not?"

"The water will come, Isbod," replied an unperturbed Moses.

At that moment the Door opened. And just beyond the Door, beside the River of Life, stood the Living God. Unnoticed by eyes that can see only the visibles, the Lord stepped out of the spiritual realm and took his place on the rock beside Moses.

Utterly unaware that the Living God was at his side, yet following his words, Moses raised his faithful rod high above his head. All Israel could see his silhouette atop the huge rock. What they could not see, but what angels beheld, was the River of Life flowing from out the throne of God, through the Door, and disappearing under the great flint rock.

That which is real is about to be pictured again for mortal eyes! thought Adorae, throwing his hands above his head in exhilaration at the unfolding scene.

Moses grasped one end of his rod in both hands. Men and angels held their breath. In that instant the Lord God stepped squarely in front of Moses even as the rod hurtled down toward the rock. To the consternation of the angels, the Lord suddenly disappeared, vanishing inside the rock.

With all his strength Moses slammed the almond rod down upon the rock. Instantly the earth contorted as the rock blurred before every eye. The ground beneath them began to rumble. A deep, subterranean earthquake had joined the smashing of the rod upon the rock. Moses was thrown to one

knee as he fought to steady himself in the presence of earth's spasms. Others also stumbled and were thrown onto the sand.

As the earth continued its fitful tremblings, a low rumble deep within the earth gradually grew into a thundering roar until every ear grew deaf, while the earth began to split asunder, fissions forming beneath the feet of Israel. The air was filled with horrendous groanings.

The flat rock suddenly cracked down the middle, from east to west, then from north to south, while a thousand lesions spread across its metallic face. The deep-throated roar continued, growing ever louder. *It is as though the earth is in labor,* thought Moses. Something deep in the bowels of the earth was battling its way to the surface. Men fell on their faces in terror. Angels exalted.

Just as the roar became unbearable, a titanic geyser broke the surface of the rock, spurted out before every watching eye, and spewed high into the air, hurtling into the sky until it pierced the clouds above, continuing its upward climb even farther until it passed higher than mortal eyes could see.

The multitude, transfixed, remained motionless.

Reaching its apex, the ascended water poured back down to earth, high winds catching it and scattering it across the throng below. A tumultuous shout rose from a million mouths as all Israel found themselves drenched in more water than had ever before fallen upon them!

Israel fell back in all directions to make room for the convulsive water as it sought out a riverbed in which to flow. At last the crystal water found its direction. Like a mighty tidal wave it surged out across the desert floor, the sand sizzling and water vaporizing as it did. The cruel desert that had known no respite for a thousand years turned cool under the bathings of this marvelous stream.

The rock's gigantic geyser gradually subsided, its waters now pouring forth through the cracks and fissures in the rock. The rock itself could not be seen for it was covered from sight by its own fountain.

The river gained momentum and disappeared over the horizon. A million people broke into a run to follow it, joined hard on by cattle, camels, barking dogs, and flocks of sheep. Two great lines of humanity spontaneously formed alongside the banks of the river, creating a scene of wild ecstasy that stretched from horizon to horizon as God's people dipped their hands into the water, bathed their hot faces, and drank their fill . . . all this in the midst of tumultuous shouts of joy and praise.

Complete strangers, finding themselves waist deep in water, began hugging one another. Children were soon in water fights. Everywhere was the sound of laughter. Along the water's edge, many broke into a dance. God's people had marched out into the most unforgiving wasteland on the face of the earth, there to meet the hand of a God different from all the gods of earth.

Israel was thirsty no more.

All through the evening and night Israel drank deep of the crystal waters that came from the sundered rock. The next morning, refreshed once more, Israel found its heart for God.

And in the heavens the recording angel, perhaps not quite as sober as usual, entered the following observation. "Earth shall see the day when this dull picture becomes bright reality."

Moses was grateful for the Lord's provision. But he continued to contemplate the waiting desert. "Half of my question has been answered. Food we have today. Water we have today, but what of all our tomorrows?"

CHAPTER
Twenty-Seven

Early the next morning Israel struck its tents. Skins and jugs were filled to the brim as they moved out across the desert floor toward a mountain of which Moses had told them. A mountain called Sinai. By evening the rock had disappeared behind them.

Morning again made its hot debut as a pitiless sun boiled down on a homeless nation trudging across an unshielded desert.

Not many such days passed until Israel was once more out of water. Faces began to blister and lips to crack. Cattle failed, children cried. A deeper hopelessness than ever descended on this vagabond nation. On that particular afternoon an exhausted nation pitched its tents and tried, vainly, to find even a slight escape from the heat under the shelter of their black tents.

In one of those tents sat Cordinel, her head resting on the center post of the tent while she held her child, who slept fitfully in her arms. The heat beat down on the tent with unabated fury.

"No child has any business being out here. Will he

survive? Perhaps Joshua and I should never have married. I never dreamed he would become a leader of Israel, so tied to the work. I so rarely see him. Whatever beauty he saw in me will soon vanish out here. Will he love me then? My child suffers so from the heat. And the land of promise lies forever from here. Lord, I am so discouraged. Were we mad to leave Egypt?"

Exhausted and despondent, with hot sweat bathing her face and her body screaming for relief, Cordinel gave in to despair.

"So very, very tired, so needy, so thirsty. Where are you Lord?" she whispered.

Cordinel lifted her head. A strange sound . . . an illusion, surely, like a desert mirage. *But is this a mirage?* she wondered. *The sound is growing louder.* Cordinel looked down at her feet, watching in amazement as a little stream of water came coursing past her tent. It flowed on, but not until it had formed a pool of water right in front of her tent.

Laying down her son, Cordinel dropped to her knees, cupped her hands, and scooped the water into her palms. It was so cool. But more amazing, it bubbled in her hands. She drank and drank again. Never had a daughter of Israel tasted such water, and never had Cordinel been so quickly refreshed. In a moment she had laid a damp cloth to the head of her sleeping child, and as she did, she raised her face toward heaven.

"You are really not at all like I thought. We have misunderstood you, have we not?"

Not far away two men bent over an open furnace, trying to create a primitive smelter to produce iron, for in Egypt it was a skill that slaves had never been allowed to learn. Try as they might, the secret of iron had eluded them. Their faces red, their throats parched, their skin burned by the furnace and the heat, the two men stepped back from the flames and collapsed, unshaded, on the hot desert.

"I would vow that I just heard the sound of a river."

"A little less than likely, though I admit I hear it too."

"Look! A stream! It is coming this way!"

In a moment, a trench of water flowed beside them. Laughing with glee, the two men rolled over into the water, drank and soaked, and wondered how water had managed to reach a place so forsaken.

And at the front of the encampment, Isbod sat down beside Moses to broach a difficult subject.

"You have so many problems to deal with. I am sorry to disturb you," apologized Isbod.

Moses sat exhausted under the tormenting inferno that was destroying the nation seeking to cross this hellatious wilderness. He raised his hand to his temples, running his fingers through his long gray locks. Bowing his head, he remained silent for a long time.

"What is it, Isbod?"

"I just wanted you to know you need to replace me. I cannot go any farther. Life is gone out of me. I will be staying here."

Moses lifted his head with a jerk. Ignoring Isbod entirely, he snapped to his feet.

"The sound of water? And laughter? Have I gone mad?"

"Quite likely!" chuckled Isbod hoarsely.

A small wave of water was flowing toward them. It was only as deep as two spans of a man's hand, yet it was as wide as the camp itself. Astonishment crept over Moses' leathered face, then turned to a smile. The water swept across Moses' path and on into the uncharted desert, bathing his feet as it passed.

"The water. It is everywhere, Isbod."

"When we need it, it comes," responded Isbod as he stumbled about in the water. "Moses! Water has come to hell," Isbod cried with childish glee. Then he added, "That is the end of you, jug! I will carry you no longer. No sir. Not one step farther."

The old man rubbed his wet hands over his face, looked up into the sky, and laughed. "Just like God. Yes sir, just like God."

"The rest of my question is answered," responded Moses, pointing to something on the horizon.

Just then Joshua broke into his tent. "Where is the water coming from?" asked Cordinel.

"Come, Cordinel," replied Joshua, a broad grin on his face. "See!"

"The Rock? I see the Rock! But we left the Rock behind days ago. Oh pity, have we moved in a circle?"

"No, it is *the Rock that moves!* The Rock is following us! The Rock is giving us the water of life as we go on our journey."

"Lord, you are the Rock that moves," said Cordinel, weeping and dropping to her knees.

Joshua knelt beside her.

"We will yet make it to Sinai."

CHAPTER
Twenty-Eight

Ragged mountains cast grotesque silhouettes upon the desert floor, but nothing Israel had seen looked more forbidding than the gnarled old mountain that loomed before them.

Bleak, solitary, and terrorizing, Sinai seemed to defy their approach. Every heart filled with dread, a million people slowly surrounded the base of that mysterious place called Sinai.

"Will God meet us *here* in *this* unmentionable place?" The question was asked in fear; the answer was feared even more.

"What kind of a God would live on *that* mountain?" muttered one of the elders.

All Israel was recalling a God who slew an entire army in an instant . . . and all the firstborn of a nation in one night. This mountain seemed fitting for a God like that. *Now* what might be Israel's fate as they came to the moment when they must *meet* him?

"No one can see God and live, Moses. Yet you tell

us we will meet him, and *here?*" The voice was once more that of Isbod.

"This is what he has told me, Isbod."

Moses began to move up the side of Sinai. He paused and turned.

"Elders of Israel, tell your people, 'Do not go beyond the boundary set here. Any who dares to climb Sinai will die, struck dead by the wrath of God.'"

"But you said the elders would climb this mountain and meet God," came the voice of another elder.

"Yes," replied Moses. "And that hour has come."

With those words the leaders of Israel began bidding their loved ones good-bye. Wives and children embraced their men and wept openly as they departed. One by one the elders stepped past the boundary. As they did, wives called out their last pledges of love to husbands they were certain would never be seen again. Soft crying, sobs, and muffled wails could be heard throughout the multitude. The elders, looking up at bleak Sinai, trembled visibly, their ashen faces betraying their fears. Only Moses and Isbod seemed to be at ease as they eagerly anticipated their ascent of Sinai.

Cordinel reached out and clasped her husband. "Joshua, your hands are ice cold."

"And this time yours are so very warm. It is not unlike the night of the Passover, only this time I am the one who is gripped by fear.

"You may never see me again, Cordinel. Can any man see the face of God and live? Today more than seventy men may die a fearsome death in the presence of God."

Cordinel's response was soft and gentle, almost inaudible. "No, Joshua, when you see him, it will not be as you suppose. You shall see the face of God and live. He is not as we think him to be."

Cordinel pulled herself away to look fully into Joshua's eyes. "And I shall see your face again."

"Dear lady, I trust that your words are wisdom, for they contradict all the thoughts of men."

"You will return, and you will understand him better."

Joshua smiled. "Then God shall be my salvation?"

Cordinel's wise reply was only to gently pronounce her husband's name. "Joshua."

With that, the servant of Moses turned and joined seventy other men as terrified as he.

Isbod was the first to move, climbing briskly toward the summit. The others knew there was wise purpose in the old man's actions. Because of his age, Isbod would surely be the last to reach the mountain top.

Slowly, cautiously, the others began climbing the barren slopes.

Suddenly everyone gasped. A few screamed. Coming out of nowhere, a dark cloud had descended on the top of Sinai. The arrival of this awful omen was followed by an earthquake and thunderous roars, then the terrifying sound of a bugle, the likes of which no human ears had ever heard. If that was not

enough to mortify the bravest soul, lightning began crashing through the smoke.

Israel was on its face, crying in sheer terror. Only on the face of the lovely Cordinel was there found the glow of peace and joy at the sight of such spectacular marvels.

And in the other realm . . .

CHAPTER
Twenty-Nine

The entire heavenly host had encircled the throne. The Lord rose, addressing his heavenly companions as he did.

"There is about to occur, here in heavenly places, what has never taken place before. In this hour it will come to pass that citizens of the fallen planet will step through the Door and come *here.*"

The angels, hearing these words, were not sure whether they should praise or weep, for they knew not what would happen to men if they saw the glories of heaven. And more! What would be the fate of men should they see the face of God?

Neither men nor angels knew the answer to this question both were asking.

The Lord stepped from his throne and moved toward the Door while angels stepped back to form a pathway through their midst. Approaching the Door, he held up his hand. The Door opened. For the first time since the fall of Adam, the flaming sword came to rest. Even the fierce cherubim stepped back . . . and vanished!

For the first time, the Door lay *unguarded*.

By now Moses and his frightened companions had made their way up the mountain to that place where the smoke rimmed the top of Sinai. They hesitated, then plunged forward, disappearing from the watching eyes of those below.

As they climbed, the mountainside grew steeper. From time to time the loose stones gave way, causing the climbers to stumble and slide back. What with the overhanging smoke, the precarious climbing, and the difficulty in seeing anything, the men were soon separated. Each now groped upward alone.

Far in the rear came Isbod, his hands cut and bleeding, his breath labored, but his heart still eager for God. He cared not at all that he would be the last to reach the summit . . . only that he reach it.

Each man, in his time, began to notice that there was some sort of light ahead. With intuition their only guide, each groped toward a light that was growing ever brighter as they moved upward in the smoke. Drawing near to the top, every elder had but one question: *What awaits me? And where are the others?*

Moses, in the lead, came to the mountain's crest and was the first to discover the remarkable answer. Others soon followed, also meeting their intended fate.

Isbod stopped to rest, his old eyes finding it hard to see anything clearly. *What is that light?* Finding one last surge of strength, Isbod moved feverishly forward.

"Where is everyone? They are already there, I am

sure. Why do I not hear *something?* Has God struck them all dead?"

Just as he felt he could not possibly climb any farther, Isbod reached up one last time to grasp the mountain's rocky slope. Quickly he drew back his hand.

"Wh . . . what was *that?*"

Isbod had touched something flat and very smooth.

"Stone! It is stone. Flat, smooth, cool stone! *Polished* stone! Impossible!" Isbod pulled himself up onto . . . onto what?

"This is a pavement!" He dropped to his knees to examine the stone.

"Sapphire! What is a polished sapphire pavement doing up on top of this ugly mountain?" Isbod cautiously rose to his feet. He looked all around, dumbfounded by his discovery.

"I seem to be standing in the middle of an enormous doorway."

Shielding his eyes from the smoke behind him and the light before him, Isbod strained his eyes for his companions . . . and God.

"There is a man! In the midst of all this glory, a *man!*"

Then Isbod caught the sound of shouts of laughter and praise.

"The other elders! They made it—all of them!" exclaimed Isbod, not sure if he should run wildly or tiptoe quietly into the awaiting scene.

"They are sitting down, eating . . . with . . ."

Isbod pulled himself to his full height and walked boldly into what he now realized was the other realm.

As the smoke cleared, what unfolded before Isbod was the strangest of scenes. Seventy elders and Moses . . . and the Living God . . . sitting together. And God was serving them food in the midst of unutterable glory.

Elders! Eating. Drinking. With God. *Fellowshiping* with the Almighty and Living God. Man, with God, in heavenly places. Eating!

The old gentleman chuckled as he moved to take his place.

"Just like God. Yes sir, just like God."

PART

IV

CHAPTER
Thirty

The wind howled furiously. Making their way out onto a narrow ledge, the two men almost had to shout in order to speak to one another.

"What is the name of this place?" called Joshua.

"It is a mountain range called Pisgah. We stand on a mount called Nebo." shouted Moses, speaking through cupped hands. "From here you can see all the land of promise. Look below! There. The entire encampment of Israel. Joshua, you must cross over that river, the Jordan, and lead them into the land. *The land!*"

Far, far below, stretching out for what seemed to be forever, was a beautiful land unlike anything the eyes of a man born and raised in Egypt had ever seen. And below was the whole nation of Israel, encamped but ready to move at Joshua's command.

"Except for our spies, Jacob was the last of our people to see this land," continued Moses, great tears sweeping down his face as he spoke.

"Look at the Jordan! Water! Beautiful water. And the land, just look at that land!" marveled Joshua.

"Glorious, is it not?" replied Moses, deep emotion

resonating in his voice. "See that area there? Name it Gilead. And in that direction, call it Naphtali. Oh, never mind. You will know. But look, there. The plains of Jericho. You will reach them first."

"How do you know all this?" asked Joshua in amazement.

Moses' face broke into a broad smile.

"He was here this morning. He showed me everything."

Moses' glistening eyes swept across the vast panorama before them. "The land of Abraham, Isaac, and Jacob," he whispered, tears returning to his eyes once more.

"Are you disappointed?" asked Joshua, studying the face of Moses as he spoke.

"You mean, because I will not be going in with you?"

There was a pause.

"Not anymore," Moses replied thoughtfully. "I will go there someday. My feet shall yet stand on that land. Perhaps it will be on a day even better than this."

Joshua did not respond, for he could not tell if Moses was merely being cheerful in the face of staggering disappointment or was speaking of something Joshua did not know about.

"Let us edge our way out along that ledge," shouted Moses. "Out of the wind." The two men moved carefully up a narrow ledge on the side of Mount Nebo, Moses leading the way with a sure and steady foot.

"You amaze me, Moses," said Joshua. "For a man who is a hundred and twenty years old, you are as steady as a mountain goat."

"I am a little amazed myself," responded Moses with genuine modesty. "Heat must be good for one's health," he added, laughing.

"And do not forget the manna," countered Joshua lightheartedly.

Moses laughed again, but then his face grew sober. "Joshua, the manna will disappear as soon as you cross the Jordan."

"What!" exclaimed Joshua, trying to grasp the enormity of that simple disclosure.

"Oh, you will not need the manna anymore, nor the Rock. You will not see them again. But never forget that you ate of the spiritual food and drank of the spiritual drink."

"I will always remember the sweets of the wilderness," replied Joshua.

"I was not referring to the wilderness, Joshua. I was recalling . . . I was remembering the sapphire pavement and that which we partook of in other realms.

Moses was now staring almost straight down, his piercing eyes scanning the camp below. "A million people are poised beside the Jordan. When they cross that river, do you know where they will get their food and drink?" queried Moses.

"No, I do not. Does that mean I, too, must face some murmuring?"

"The land! The land will supply you *everything.*

"As to murmuring, all who enter his work face that. But come, there is much I must tell you."

The two men talked for hours, into the evening and on into the night. And with the coming of night a hundred thousand twinkling lights sparkled in the dark below them, joined by ringlets of smoke rising from thousands of campfires.

Eventually the two men eased their way off the ledge and began their trek down the mountain slope. After several minutes, Moses stopped. A little hesitant at first, then drawing himself up, he turned to Joshua.

"Here."

There was a finality in his voice.

"I must say good-bye to you, my friend."

More quickly than he thought was possible, Joshua's eyes filled with tears. The two men fell into a long embrace, weeping freely. Abruptly Moses brought Joshua up with a strong arm.

"You must go; it is late. There is little light tonight. Here, I have something to give you." Moses pointed to something he had left behind on their upward climb.

Moses pulled forth a large leather bag, hard and cracked by age and heat. Joshua knew its contents well, for he had often watched Moses reach into it, bring forth a scroll, and make an entry.

"Take it. I have sealed all the scrolls. That is, I have sealed all but one, the last." With these words Moses unrolled the one unprotected scroll.

"I have kept a small space at the end of this one. It is for you. I think you might want to write the ending to today's story. Do so when you arrive back at camp."

"Moses, I must ask. The rock, the last time you struck it, you struck it inappropriately. But why were you not allowed to enter the land because of hitting the rock?"

"Perhaps . . ." Moses' words came slow and labored. "Perhaps it was not a rock that I struck."

Joshua knew that would be the extent of Moses' explanation.

Moses turned to go.

"Wait! One last question. What have you learned of God that above all else is central in your thoughts?"

Moses smiled. "You mean *besides* the fact that people have a very hard time obeying the Law? So hard a time that I sometimes wonder if it is possible for them to do so. Beyond that . . . one thing!"

"What?"

"In."

"Did you say, 'In'?"

"Yes, *in*."

Joshua knew he was to say no more. Moses would pursue the thought if he chose to.

"There are things . . . things in the heavens . . . not known here."

Joshua waited.

"Creation is *in* him."

Joshua bit his lip.

"He came into his creation."

The biting of his lip was insufficient. Joshua switched to biting his tongue.

"He came into the garden. As Eve was hidden in Adam, I cannot but believe there is yet a mystery hidden *in* God.

"Our Lord came into the tabernacle. And he will be *in* the land.

"He appeared to me in a bush, in light and smoke, and in human form.

"There is more. Death does not know, nor sin, nor the enemy. There is a mystery, Joshua, one we cannot comprehend. I dare not consider the implications. There is another *in* waiting to be revealed out there someday. *That* is my deepest impression."

There was a long moment of silence. "Now it is time to bid you good-bye."

Moses' voice dropped, his words coming very slowly.

"By tomorrow morning, Joshua, the man Moses will be no more."

Joshua swung the bag and its precious cargo of scrolls over his shoulder. "I understand."

As Moses helped Joshua adjust the huge pack, he laughed one last time. "I write too much."

"Not enough, in my opinion," replied Joshua. "Not enough."

"Regrettably, there was not a great deal of time for

writing. I was always so taken up with the needs of the people.

"One day soon, as time permits, have a copy made of each scroll. Who knows? Perhaps someday someone will be interested in reading the story of our sojourn. And God's beginnings with us.

"One last word, Joshua. It concerns the land. We have had a lamb, and a Rock, and manna. And, of course, the instructions I received from our Lord to build a miniature replica of what we saw in the heavens. Glorious . . . glorious. Well, you know all that.

"Now, look into the valley. What you see is a nation. A nation that is an army. That tiny replica of heaven's grandest glory, the tabernacle, sits at the very center of this army-nation.

"Joshua, each of these—the manna, the Rock, the tabernacle, the lamb, the priests and their garments, even the army—all have told us something about our Lord." Looking Joshua straight in the eye, Moses continued. "None of them . . . *none* of them tell of him as completely as does the land. The land, more than anything else, teaches us about our Lord.

"Enter that land. Live on it, for it will become *absolutely everything* to you." Reaching out, Moses placed his hands firmly on Joshua's shoulders.

"Make sure his people are rooted in that land. Ground them in that land. *In* the land! All that is needed is that land."

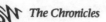

Moses took a deep breath, releasing it slowly. "With that, my brother, go."

"Are you afraid?"

"What?" responded Moses in complete surprise. "Of course not."

A pleasant thought crossed Moses' mind, his face breaking into a soft smile. "Why should I be afraid, Joshua? I have already been there several times, you know."

"Yes," grinned Joshua. "And I, *once.*"

"Then we need say no more."

Again the two men embraced. Joshua turned and started down the mountain to pursue the conquest of a vast land God had promised so long ago to one who had believed.

Moses turned and began walking away, as casually as might a man taking a quiet evening stroll. As he walked he looked about, perchance to happen upon a large Door . . . slightly ajar.

CHAPTER
Thirty-One

"Gabriel. Michael. Come with me. We shall visit the land Israel is about to enter."

With those words Michael, Gabriel, and the Living God stepped out onto a land bordering the Great Sea.

"The most important dramas of human history will be played out on this land. As you know, Abraham came first to this land. Jacob departed from it. His descendants will enter again tomorrow. One day Babylon . . ." The Lord paused. "But . . . that is another story.

"Come. I want you to see those places that will one day be known by all mankind."

The two archangels found themselves beside a river. "My people will cross here tomorrow. This river divides all things from my people. On one side is death. On the other, life."

The Lord raised his hand.

The scene changed. This time the Door came to rest in an open field, a few tents nearby. "A village shall rise here, and in this village shall a great king be born. No . . . *two* great kings shall be born here."

"Lord, it is as though you have already been here when these things happened, yet they have not happened. Have you peered into future days? Is that possible?"

"Yes, I have already been here. I have seen the end from the beginning and the beginning from the end."

"Lord, I do not understand," responded Michael.

"Nor did Recorder when I spoke the same words to him. Suffice it to be said, but not to be understood, that I *finished* all things before I *began* all things. Now come."

The scene changed again. The trio stood beside a beautiful lake. "My very words, out of my own mouth, shall be spoken here among the poor." Before Michael and Gabriel could inquire of the meaning of the strange statement, the scene abruptly changed. The two archangels found themselves standing on a peaceful hill covered with olive trees. At the base of the hill was a small stream and beyond that a knoll.

"A great city will rise just beyond that stream. That city will be the center of all that I have planned from the beginning . . . and all that I purposed *before* the beginning. You will both come to this place on important occasions."

The two archangels said nothing, expecting the scene to change again. Instead, the Lord stepped onto the ground and began to walk toward the olive-covered hill. The two archangels sensed that their Lord had chosen a moment of solitude.

A dreadful sadness crept over the Lord's face as he gazed at a particular place on the side of the hill.

"It is here, in this cursed place, that I will put an end to all things," he whispered. "The entire creation will *end,* here. All things that are not in me shall be annihilated on this hill."

The Lord moved farther across the hill and paused again. He now stood beside a mass of solid rock protruding from the hill. The two archangels heard their Lord's voice ring clearly.

"Hear me, my enemy! This shall become a place of tombs. But it is also *here* that I shall begin again. It is here that I shall make all things new! Here I shall cause to come into existence a new creation, replacing this one . . . which I have vowed to destroy."

The Lord faced Michael and Gabriel again. "To this vast and rich land Abraham came. From out of his loins will come a seed. And from that seed shall come *triumph* over all that is the fall!"

Having spoken those words, the Lord passed back through the Door and returned to his throne, his eyes glistening fire.

"Tomorrow shall begin the battle for the land. We shall see, Lucifer, just who is lord of earth!"

CHAPTER
Thirty-Two

"It is as you said," spoke Cordinel, now in her sixtieth year yet still remarkably beautiful. "There is no manna this morning."

"As Moses said . . ." began Joshua, reflecting as he stared out upon the verdant fields that lay before him. "Three days ago we celebrated the Passover. Yesterday we ate manna. But never again. Henceforth the land alone shall provide us *everything*."

Turning to the beautiful woman he had fallen in love with in his youth, he inquired, "What shall be our fare this good morning? What is it that the land has provided?"

"All day yesterday men and women went throughout the land, up into the hills, down in the valleys, and across endless fields searching out the riches of the land," replied Cordinel.

"And what have they found?"

"This morning you and I and all of Israel shall have our first non-manna breakfast in nearly forty years. This meal also marks the first breakfast, and the first food, to be eaten on this soil by a Hebrew in hundreds of years."

Joshua sniffed the air. "I can smell the aroma. From where does it come?"

"From the slope of a small hill not far from here. I believe a few of your friends are expecting you," replied Cordinel with an air of mischievousness and delight. "Come! Your friends are all so excited, Joshua! They want so much for you to see what they have found *in* the land."

It was a pensive Joshua who responded to her words. "On a third day, long ago, he gave us water. And now on a third day he has given us the land. Oh, the riches to be found on the third day."

"Before we go . . ." Joshua softly touched Cordinel's cheeks. "I cannot believe how well you have kept your years."

He who created beauty
made of you her daughter.
And both do time defy.
For in her presence
dost thou beauty
beautify.
Before thy fairness
age does nought but stand aloof.
Thy passing years disguise
themselves in youth.

Joshua took Cordinel by the hand, and together

they strolled up a small knoll. Thousands of columns of smoke showed that an entire nation was dining from the abundance of the land!

"We gather strength for a new march. And for battle," Joshua said quietly, as he watched Hebrew men dressed in soldiers' uniforms pass by.

"The land has given food and drink and strength to a nation . . . and raised an army in a day."

Just then Joshua caught sight of a lavish spread of food laid out on the ground.

Joshua greeted his friends warmly. Several told him stories of where the food had been found and of their discoveries of the abundance and riches of the land. There was excitement in every voice.

As Joshua seated himself among his friends, he found himself choking back a sob. "This reminds me of . . ."

At that moment one of the young soldiers interrupted. "Do you have a word for the army?"

"Yes. After the men have eaten and drunk, they will have gained the strength of an army. At that time all tribes will assemble, each tribe at its designated place. Now watch the sun. Prepare to sound the ram's horn the moment the sun breaks over that mountain range."

"Prince of Ephraim," came a voice.

Joshua turned. It was Cordinel, calling him by a name she rarely used. She was smiling, tears in her eyes, pride upon her face.

"Enough of business. Eat the fruit of this rich, rich land."

For a moment Joshua could do nothing but stare at the food. Not in forty years of travel nor in all the years in Egypt had he seen such variety and abundance.

"Lavish. He has lavished his riches on us. Moses, if only you could be here now." Joshua's voice wavered as he spoke. "Surely leaving Egypt was worth this meal alone.

"Lush green grass everywhere, and resting here on it . . . lentils, cucumbers, beans, pomegranates, figs and grapes, roasted barley and wheat, with millet cakes. All of this and curds, milk, and honey, a huge platter of olives the like of which we have never seen. And at the center, a roasted calf. What a sight!"

Cordinel's voice, filled with emotion, joined in, "It is a rich land, my husband!"

"More than rich," he replied, still staring at the food, almost in unbelief. "As I was about to say, it is not unlike a banquet I once attended."

Everyone fell quiet, for all knew that no slave of Egypt nor wilderness wanderer had *ever* seen a meal like this.

"Oh! Never mind. I was referring to something that happened in another . . . well . . . some other place."

"What? Where?" asked a friend, realizing Joshua was referring to something he had never spoken of before.

"Uh . . . on a sapphire pavement. Before the throne of God."

Joshua cleared his throat and once more swept

tears from his eyes. "In a few moments you will hear the sounding of a ram's horn. Together we will march forward to explore the heights, the depths, the breadth, and the length of the riches of this land. In so doing the land will reveal to us much of the height and depth and breadth of the riches of our Lord."

With those words spoken, there came the sound of a ram's horn.

CHAPTER
Thirty-Three

"They are about to move forward," cried Michael.

"Every angel to his legion," shouted Gabriel.

The Door swung wide. Thousands upon thousands of angels swept through the portal and stepped out upon the grassy fields of Palestine. Legion upon legion came the angels while, just beyond them, the army of Israel was assembling.

In that moment the Lord also stepped out onto the land, watching Israel's army form, tribe by tribe.

Unseen by any earthly eye, a living sea of angels divided, making room for Israel to pass through their midst. The angelic host now surrounded the entire nation of Israel! Not one son or daughter of Jacob knew the mightiest army in creation was around about them.

"Joshua shall lead the visible army, and our Lord shall lead us," observed Adorae to his companion, referring to the ragtag army of the Hebrews and the angelic warriors of heaven.

Standing before the army and all the people, Joshua cried out.

Garlic and leeks of Egypt.
Manna of the desert.
A Rock that followed us.
We thank you, O God.
And for a lamb.
And for this land.

"Now, hear, O Israel!" he cried again.

In the distance came once more the haunting blare of a ram's horn to which *two* armies fully responded.

"The tribes are assembled, Joshua!" cried one of his men. "The ark in the midst. Judah in the lead."

"We are ready to enter the land," spoke both Joshua and the Lord simultaneously.

The mighty shout of a million human voices thundered, joined by a thousand thousand exuberant shouts of praise from the angelic host.

With the walls of a fortified city lying at a distance before him, Joshua walked to the front of the tribe of Judah. Suddenly he halted, his right hand going instantly to his sword.

There is someone out there. What is that man? Is he of good or of evil?

"Who are you?" Joshua called aloud.

The one to whom he called, his silhouette captured on the horizon, was a very imposing man indeed, standing regal and fearless yet all alone . . . or so it seemed to human eyes.

Because of the distance between them, Joshua

could not be sure if the man was facing him or looking out toward Jericho.

Joshua advanced toward the man, his sword partially unsheathed. As Joshua approached, he could see that the mysterious stranger had drawn his sword and was holding it high above his head, its blade glistening in the morning sun.

The man's back was to Joshua, his face set like flint toward Jericho.

There was something in the stance of this man—his boldness, his bearing, the aura of authority—that caused Joshua to know that this man was in command of an army.

Joshua stopped, unsheathed his sword, and cried defiantly, "Are you for us or for the enemy?" The man turned around. Joshua dropped his sword.

"I know you. You are no enemy of mine."

"No, I am not your enemy, Joshua."

The man raised his hand. Joshua gasped.

For one bright instant, Joshua could see as God sees. All around him—and around all Israel—stood an army unlike anything this earth had ever seen or known.

"All heaven is here," stammered Joshua.

The strange man, a stranger no longer, spoke again.

I am the Captain of this host.
Be strong, Joshua.

As I was with Moses,
so shall I be with you.
You will take this land
I promised.
No one will stand against you.
I will never forsake you.
And where your foot falls,
there will you conquer.
Only take courage and be strong.

Joshua grabbed for his shoes and pulled them from
his feet, for he stood upon holy ground.

EPILOGUE

On that day the sons and daughters of Jacob marched into that land so holy. And there they dwelt for over a thousand years. Many marvelous and wonderful events occurred during that millennium, but none quite so glorious as the escape from Egypt.

That is, none until a woman of middle age, long past her childbearing years, lifted her face toward heaven and pleaded with her Lord to give her a son.

And it was not until the Lord answered that woman's prayer that human eyes beheld an event that would eclipse even *the escape,* for that prayer set in motion events that would culminate in creation's greatest marvel, *the birth.*

SeedSowers
P.O. Box 3317, Jacksonville, FL 32206
800-228-2665   fax 904-598-3456
www.seedsowers.com

REVOLUTIONARY BOOKS ON CHURCH LIFE

How to Meet In Homes (*Edwards*) 10.95
An Open Letter to House Church Leaders (*Edwards*) 4.00
When the Church Was Led Only by Laymen *(Edwards)* 4.00
Beyond Radical (*Edwards*) 5.95
Rethinking Elders (*Edwards*) 9.95
Revolution, The Story of the Early Church (*Edwards*) 8.95
The Silas Diary (*Edwards*) 9.99
The Titus Diary (*Edwards*) 8.99
The Timothy Diary (*Edwards*) 9.99
The Priscilla Diary (*Edwards*) 9.99
The Gaius Diary *(Edwards)* 10.99
Overlooked Christianity (*Edwards*) 14.95
Pagan Christianity *(Viola)* 13.95

AN INTRODUCTION TO THE DEEPER CHRISTIAN LIFE

Living by the Highest Life (*Edwards*) 10.99
The Secret to the Christian Life (*Edwards*) 8.99
The Inward Journey (*Edwards*) 8.99

CLASSICS ON THE DEEPER CHRISTIAN LIFE

Experiencing the Depths of Jesus Christ (*Guyon*) 8.95
Practicing His Presence (*Lawrence/Laubach*) 8.95
The Spiritual Guide (*Molinos*) 8.95
Union With God (*Guyon*) 8.95
The Seeking Heart (*Fenelon*) 9.95
Intimacy with Christ (*Guyon*) 10.95
The Song of the Bride *(Guyon)* 9.95
Spiritual Torrents (*Guyon*) 10.95
The Ultimate Intention (*Fromke*) 11.00

IN A CLASS BY ITSELF

The Divine Romance (*Edwards*) 8.95

NEW TESTAMENT

The Story of My Life as Told by Jesus Christ *(Four gospels blended)* 14.95
Acts in First Person *(Book of Acts)* 9.95

COMMENTARIES BY JEANNE GUYON

Genesis Commentary 10.95
Exodus Commentary 10.95
Leviticus - Numbers - Deuteronomy Commentaries 14.95
Judges Commentary 7.95
Job Commentary 10.95
Song of Songs *(Song of Solomon Commentary)* 9.95
Jeremiah Commentary 7.95
James - I John - Revelation Commentaries 14.95

Prices subject to change

The Chronicles of Heaven *(Edwards)*

The Beginning 8.99
The Escape 8.99
The Birth 8.99
The Triumph 8.99
The Return 8.99

The Collected works of T. Austin-Sparks

The Centrality of Jesus Christ 19.95
The House of God 29.95
Ministry 29.95
Service 19.95
Spiritual Foundations 29.95
The Things of the Spirit 10.95
Prayer 14.95
The On-High Calling 10.95
Rivers of Living Water 8.95
The Power of His Resurrection 8.95

Comfort and Healing

A Tale of Three Kings *(Edwards)* 8.99
The Prisoner in the Third Cell *(Edwards)* 5.99
Letters to a Devastated Christian *(Edwards)* 7.95
Exquisite Agony *(Edwards)* 8.95
Dear Lillian *(Edwards)* 5.95

Other books on Church Life

Climb the Highest Mountain *(Edwards)* 12.95
The Torch of the Testimony *(Kennedy)* 14.95
The Passing of the Torch *(Chen)* 9.95
Going to Church in the First Century *(Banks)* 5.95
When the Church was Young *(Loosley)* 8.95
Church Unity *(Litzman,Nee,Edwards)* 10.95
Rethinking the Wineskin *(Viola)* 8.95
Who is Your Covering? *(Viola)* 6.95
Let's Return to Christian Unity *(Kurosaki)* 10.95

Christian Living

The Autobiography of Jeanne Guyon 19.95
Final Steps in Christian Maturity *(Guyon)* 12.95
Turkeys and Eagles *(Lord)* 8.95
The Life of Jeanne Guyon *(T.C. Upham)* 17.95
Life's Ultimate Privilege *(Fromke)* 10.00
Unto Full Stature *(Fromke)* 10.00
All and Only *(Kilpatrick)* 7.95
Adoration *(Kilpatrick)* 8.95
Release of the Spirit *(Nee)* 9.99
Bone of His Bone *(Huegel)* modernized 8.95
One Hundred Days in the Secret Place *(Edwards)* 12.99

Prices subject to change

The Chronicles of Heaven
by
Gene Edwards

The Old Testament

The Beginning covers *Genesis*, chapters 1&2 (*The Promise* will come next, covering the rest of *Genesis*). *The Escape*, already in print, covers *Exodus*. Other volumes will follow until the Pentateuch is finished.

In *The Beginning* God creates the heavens and the earth. The crowning glory of creation is man and woman, who live and move in both the visible world and the spiritual world.

Experience one of the greatest events of human history: *The Escape* of the Israelite people from Egypt. Watch the drama from that of earthly participants and that of the angels in the heavens.

Experience the wonderful story of the incarnation, the Christmas story, seen from both realms. *The Birth* introduces the mystery of the Christian life for those who have never heard the story.

The New Testament

The Chronicles then extend into the *New Testament*. They are *The Birth* and *The Triumph*. After *The Triumph* comes *The First Century Diaries* !

In *The Triumph* you will experience the Easter story as you never have before. Join angels as they comprehend the suffering and death of Jesus and the mystery of free will in light of God's Eternal Purpose.

The Door. It has moved to a hill on Patmos. What would John be allowed to see? Come along and witness the finale of the stirring conclusion to *The Chronicles of Heaven.*

100 DAYS
IN THE
SECRET PLACE

BORED WITH THE EXERCISES OF RELIGIOUS RITUALISM and parched by dry teachings, man searches for a way back to the place of His presence.

GENE EDWARDS, THE MASTER STORYTELLER, HAS gathered together the writings of three of history's greatest Christians. Michael Molinos, Jeanne Guyon, and Francois Fenelon show you the way to the secret place where searching ends. The writings of these "masters of the spiritual way" will be as lampposts leading the weary traveler towards that secret place lovingly prepared by the Father.

THE WRITINGS OF MOLINOS, GUYON, AND FENELON call you to step over the threshold into a place where God has prepared for you to live.

Living in a drought of spiritual dryness,
Lost in the depths of spiritual loneliness,
Are you longing for a moment of spiritual reality?

Then *100 Days in the Secret Place* is for you!

The First-Century Diaries

by
Gene Edwards

I.

The Silas Diary

This historical narrative parallels the book of Acts, giving a first-person account of Paul's first journey.

The Silas Diary is your invitation to join Silas, Paul, and their companions on a journey fraught with danger and adventure – a journey that changed the history of the world. Learn with the first-century Christians what freedom in Christ really means.

II.

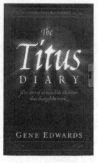

The Titus Diary

This compelling narrative continues the events of the book of Acts. *The Titus Diary* is a firsthand account of Paul's second journey as told by Titus.

Join this journey as Paul sets out once more–this time with Silas, Timothy, and Luke–and learn of the founding of the churches in Philippi, Thessalonica, Corinth, and Ephesus. Look on as Paul meets Aquila and Priscilla and quickly gains an appreciation of their passion for the Lord and his church.

III.

The Timothy Diary

In *The Timothy Diary* Paul's young Christian companion, Timothy, gives a firsthand account of Paul's third journey.

This journey is quite different from Paul's others. It is the fulfillment of Paul's dream, for in Ephesus Paul trains a handful of young men to take his place after his death. Paul follows Christ's example in choosing and training disciples to spread the gospel and encourage the growth of the church.

The First-Century Diaries

IV.

The Priscilla Diary

Here are the stories of Paul's continued travels to the first-century churches narrated from the unique perspective of Priscilla, a vibrant first-century Christian woman!

See Paul writing his most personally revealing letter, his letter to the church in Corinth. Marvel at the truths Paul conveys to the church in Rome, a letter "of all that Paul considered central to the Christian life."

V.

The Gaius Diary

Paul and Nero meet face to face in a moment of highest drama.

Paul is released, but soon is arrested again, and again faces Nero. The sentence is death. Just before his execution, all the men he trained arrived in Rome to be with him. *The Gaius Diary* gives life changing insight into Paul's final letters. Colossians, Ephesians, Philemon, and Philippians come alive as you see in living color the background to these letters. Be there in April of 70 A.D. when Jerusalem is destroyed.

If you never read any other books on the New Testament...
Read *The First-Century Diaries!*
More than what you would learn in Seminary!

The Divine Romance

by
Gene Edwards

The Divine Romance is praised as one of the all-time literary achievements of the Protestant era. Breathtakingly beautiful, here is the odyssey of Christ's quest for His bride. *The Divine Romance* is the most captivating, heartwarming and inspirational romance that transcends space and time. In all of Christian literature there has never been a description of the crucifixion and resurrection which rivals the one depicted in *The Divine Romance*.

Many readers have commented, "This book should come with a box of Kleenex." The description of the romance between Adam and Eve alone is one of the great love stories of all times.

Edwards' portrayal of the romance of Christ and His bride takes its place along side such classics as Dante's *The Divine Comedy* and Milton's *Paradise Lost*. Reading this literary masterpiece will alter your life forever.

One of the greatest Christian classics of all-time.

Books that Heal

Exquisite Agony
(formerly titled *Crucified by Christians*)

Gene Edwards

Here is healing for hurting and disillusioned Christians who have known the pain of betrayal at the hand of another believer.

This book has brought restoration to Christians all over the world who had lost all hope. Edwards takes you to a high place to see your pain and suffering from the viewpoint of the Lord.

Read this book and learn the *privilege of betrayal* and discover who the real author of your crucifixion is!

Letters to a Devastated Christian

Gene Edwards

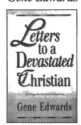

The Christian landscape is covered with the remains of lives ruined at the hands of authoritarian movements. Some believers never recover. Others are the walking wounded.

In *Letters to a Devastated Christian,* Edwards has written a series of letters to a brokenhearted Christian and points him to healing in Christ. This book is full of profound healing and hope.

The Prisoner in the Third Cell

Gene Edwards

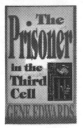

This is a book of comfort, told as an unforgettable drama, for those caught up in circumstances of life they do not understand.

In this dramatic story, John the Baptist, imprisoned by Herod and awaiting death, struggles to understand a Lord who did not live up to his expectations.

If you are a suffering Christian or know of one, this book will bring enormous comfort and insight into the ways of God.

A Tale of Three Kings
Gene Edwards

Many Christians have experienced pain, loss and heartache at the hands of other believers. To those believers, this compelling story offers comfort, healing and hope.

This simple, powerful, and beautiful story has been recommended by Christians throughout the world.

This tale is based on the biblical figures of David, Saul, and Absalom.